THE AUCTION BLOCK

BY CICELY R. JAUBERT

DORRANCE
PUBLISHING CO
EST. 1920
PITTSBURGH, PENNSYLVANIA 15238

The contents of this work, including, but not limited to, the accuracy of events, people, and places depicted; opinions expressed; permission to use previously published materials included; and any advice given or actions advocated are solely the responsibility of the author, who assumes all liability for said work and indemnifies the publisher against any claims stemming from publication of the work.

Dorrance Publishing Co
585 Alpha Drive
Suite 103
Pittsburgh, PA 15238
Visit our website at *www.dorrancebookstore.com*

ISBN: 978-1-4809-1152-9
eISBN: 978-1-4809-1474-2

CHAPTER ONE

Some people living on the other side of prison walls think confinement is a remedy for people who break rules. They think confinement is a means for controlling illegal behavior. They think separating people who have issues from other people who don't have the same issues corrects the problems. However, confinement and isolation do not rid a person of his or her anger management issues, identity crisis, or socioeconomic woes. Confinement does not eradicate depression, self-loathing, drug addiction, racial prejudice, or illiteracy. Confinement merely presents an inmate with an opportunity to face himself and accept responsibility for his past actions, make better choices for his future, or waste more time doing nothing. In the latter case, confinement would only intensify the problems because isolating volatile people in a vacuum with themselves or other volatile people is like giving them a can of gasoline and a box of matches. Dysfunctional people cannot change themselves, so when society separates them and houses them in cages with other dysfunctional people in an unnatural, controlled, dysfunctional environment, they absorb the other forms of dysfunction they are exposed to in that environment; they become even worse after their time in prison than they were before they became incarcerated. Even so, we can't allow these crimes to go unpunished just because they are dysfunctional, and if we don't separate them from mainstream society, then our communities, financial institutions, social organizations, churches, government agencies, and so on will remain polluted by crime. Isolation and confinement may not be the best answer, but it's the only one we have, and it is effective but not always in a positive way.

I have personally seen the negative psychological effects of prolonged confinement and isolation. The process is like watching a garment slowly unravel as a single piece of loose thread is pulled from the hem. Over time, the finished garment becomes less recognizable and appears to be more like a pile of meaningless threads that were never purposely sewn together. When the unraveling process is finished, the threads can never be woven back together exactly as they were and what remains of the garment is unusable. Involuntary prolonged isolation and confinement gradually depletes human nature and forces people to form unnatural attachments to inanimate objects.

During the first stage, inmates busy themselves with books, crafts, and other hobbies to keep the lack of human contact from cracking the psychological cement holding the walls of their sanity together. Once the walls have been breached, the inmates assign names, faces, and personality traits to objects so they can retain the memories — good and bad — they have of people. During the second phase, their own human self-preservation kicks in, and the objects they personified before become unequal substitutes for humans; they create companions they eat, sleep, bathe, argue, and have sex with to continue engaging in typical human behavior. It is not uncommon to see an inmate fighting with their companion. The only problem is that the companion is invisible and exists only in that inmate's imagination. When the imaginary companions begin to fade, the inmate becomes self-destructive and eventually withdraws from everything that encompasses life, which is stage three. The inmate continues to age, and all the layers of his youth, vitality, and creativity are peeled away like a banana peel year by year until eventually he is dead while he yet lives. Thus, he becomes institutionalized and now needs incarceration to continue existing.

People, like spools of thread, are deliberately interwoven by genealogy, common causes, income, intellect, religious convictions, public policies, and even problems. We are wonderfully intertwined like individual patches on a patchwork quilt. Each individual patch is different, but all the patches are needed to make the quilt a finished product. When a patch is cut out of the quilt, it leaves a hole in the quilt that can only be replaced with another patch. The single patch, however, becomes useless alone, and its purpose for existing is taken away. Like the lone patch, an isolated and confined human becomes useless when his or her ability to contribute to and receive from the lives of other humans is cut off. Whatever his or her purpose is will never be fulfilled until the person is reunited with humanity. But if they are isolated and confined too long, a reunion with humanity in the free world would be detrimental; the former inmate would be so far behind the rest of the free world that unless he has a strong chain of support and a viable skill, formal education, or amazing talent, he won't survive.

On the other hand, isolation and confinement can also be good things when we are isolated by purpose. For example, college students isolate themselves when they need to study for their classes. Writers often isolate themselves when they are working on their manuscripts. Entertainers isolate themselves for rehearsals. Parishioners isolate themselves when they are communing with God. Some people, in general, isolate themselves when they need to weigh their options before making a major decision. Many times, vacations are taken in places that are considered isolated or less populated. The idea is to get away from masses of people. But self-imposed isolation is different because we are always able to reunite with other humans whenever we want to. It's the union between isolation and confinement that creates a potentially lethal situation. As strange as it may sound, though, I know just as many people who are isolated and confined but not physically incarcerated.

Shortly after I started working at the prison, I personally decided to attend some Addicts Anonymous meetings to get a better understanding of an addict's mentality since I would be dealing with them at work. The first few meetings I attended were a bit overwhelming for me. We see the lives of addicts played out through fictional characters on television and in film, but we never suspect we'll ever come face to face with a real person who was so high that he or she put his or her child in an oven and killed the child. Most of the images we see of addicts are stereotypes, but not all addicts are uneducated, poor, or unemployed people using their addiction to certain vices to mask their feelings of entitlement or unrequited respect. In fact, most addicts in AA have jobs and maintain longevity with their employment so they can continue supporting their habits. That being said, the meetings are structured with scheduled breaks, and sometimes the participants collectively bring food and other snacks to munch on, which makes talking about one's inner-self with a group of strangers a little easier. We position our chairs in a circle, so we can face each other when we're talking. Each participant is free to share whatever experiences he or she wants to share that may be related to or the result of the addiction, and there is absolutely no judgment for whatever is said because everyone there is addicted to something.

One night in one of the meetings, a man named John decided to lead the discussion with his addiction to cocaine and alcohol. John was a tall, thin man with a heavy frame. He should have been and used to be a lot heavier, but years of snorting cocaine and drinking shriveled him. John was fifty-two with dark hair that was beginning to recede at the crest of his head. He was clean-shaven and neatly dressed. He had big black eyes that were deeply set into their sockets, surrounded by bags underneath them and bushy eyebrows on top of them. He had a long pointed nose that had been distorted. Years of snorting cocaine damaged the tissue in his nose that separated his nostrils from each other. The ingredients in the cocaine had worn the tissue away, which is one of the reasons why "snorters" often have nosebleeds or runny noses. John crossed his legs, cleared his throat, and started speaking about the career he had as an accountant when he was first introduced to cocaine.

John had been divorced for nearly eight years and hadn't really dated. He was very successful but had no real social life because he kept himself buried in his work. One evening, one of his colleagues invited him to a party thrown by one of the business associates in a firm his company represented. John didn't normally make appearances at social events outside of work, but he decided to go this time more so to shut up some of his co-workers who had been bugging him about the party all week. He arrived in attire he would normally wear to work — a dark suit and tie — and made his way to an unoccupied corner in the room that he spotted when he came through the front door. Within a few moments, his obnoxious, intoxicated co-workers saw him and staggered to him with a drink and an informal invitation to go outside to the pool area in the backyard.

When they got outside, there were a few people gathered around a lawn table giggling and laughing, including the host of the party. When John and his co-workers finally reached the table, the host handed him a one hundred dollar bill that had been rolled into a straw. John wasn't sure of what to do just then, but when the people around the table backed up, he saw the lines of cocaine that were separated in rows on the table and the razor they used to separate them. The onlookers jeered, "snort, snort, snort," so he did. That one line changed his life forever, and he became a functioning cocaine addict who worked hard by day but got high at night. John later became an alcoholic to drown his sorrows after snorting for nearly two days one weekend.

He left his house to go to the supermarket, which was less than miles away. He was so high, he ran a stop sign and killed a twelve-year-old boy on his bicycle. John has seen that boy every day since the accident four years ago and has never forgiven himself. The accident left him in a psychological prison with bars made of guilt. As one might expect, his company fired him after the accident was published in the local newspaper. John was always frugal with his money, so he wasn't in dire need of immediate employment. Since he was so ashamed of what had happened, he would rarely leave his house or even come outside. His once well-manicured yard had become an unkempt yard full of overgrown weeds, and his trash began to pile up because he didn't take it out frequently for fear of someone seeing him. John literally stayed in his house all day, drinking himself to an early grave. It was only after he read a leaflet about the redemptive power of Jesus that was left in his door by a stranger who distributed them throughout his neighborhood that John finally sought help. But John was only one of many people in that place who was isolated and confined by problems they thought were insurmountable. Everybody in there had a larger-than-life story behind his or her eyes.

After about a month of AA, I even started thinking about my own life and about why I was so reclusive outside of work myself. What kind of mask was I really wearing in everyday life and whom was I hiding from? I began to search my own memories to see if I had any unresolved problems that I kept buried inside me somewhere. I started seriously thinking about why it was so much easier to live among strangers for me than it was to live around my own family and why I spent the majority of my time alone. Taking inventory of my own life made me realize I was just as isolated and confined as the people in the AA meetings and the inmates I worked with. We were all dysfunctional peas being housed in pods with problems. What made us different was how we chose to respond to those problems.

I continued attending the AA meetings to gain more insight into the world of addiction and to also help myself. Every meeting was therapeutic yet precarious because you had to make yourself vulnerable to people you had no deeply rooted trust in. You had to expose yourself in ways that left you feeling publicly unveiled, which was uncomfortable but necessary if you wanted to overcome your issues. I had also gained some valuable intervention skills I had already put to use at work with some of the newer inmates who were addicts before they arrived. One of the most difficult events to witness is an inmate going through stages of withdrawal, especially from drug addiction. However, the AA meetings helped me to understand what happens to addicts physically and psychologically when they are trying to break the habit. It's a painful process, but with support and encouragement, it can be done.

Aside from this, attending AA keeps me from working too much. I have always been a workaholic who didn't always know when to take a vacation, and I have a tendency to bring my work home, which often becomes too involving. You would think I would stop doing this, knowing I am going end up combing my brain with a fine-tooth comb searching for answers about why this inmate said or did this and why that inmate said or did that. Many of my coworkers tell me I expend too much time and energy with my job because I am primarily supposed to teach English. I know this and I love what I do, but I also believe that information still has the ability to change people. I suppose I get so frustrated sometimes because I am still waiting for the change to take place in many of the inmates who attend my class. The frustration I feel leads to lingering insomnia at times, and I have been fighting with it for the last three or four days.

I have been tossing and turning in bed unable to sleep the last few nights, thinking about something a new inmate in my class said in our last session. It has been many years since silence nagged me so much that I couldn't sleep, but something was really disturbing to me about the offhanded comment he made in my classroom. I wasn't exactly sure if I was offended by what he said or how he said it, or perhaps it was the relevance of the comment as it pertained to incidents currently happening in the prison. All I know is that I didn't like it; I couldn't mentally release it, and the sound of nothing was so loud in my bedroom I actually wanted some other sound to slice through it, so I could stop thinking about the comment and allow the other sound to function as a lullaby. Nights like these really concern me because something serious is always behind them. I usually end up getting out of bed to record my thoughts in a notebook, so whenever something happens, I have a point of reference I can go back to. I can't readily say what is really on my mind, but I know it has something to do with my job in relation to the comment. Whatever it is, is causing me to lie awake in bed night after night before my alarm goes off, pondering the infinite possibilities of "what if." I lie here thinking about everything and nothing all at the same time. That sounds like a ridiculous oxymoron, but I can say with fair certainty that you can't easily dismiss everything you hear in the prison, but you can't allow yourself to be completely engulfed by rumors or threats either.

I suppose the danger and complexity of my job is enough to make anybody lose sleep. My work world consists of iron bars, cement walls, bulletproof glass, automatic weapons, and steel tables and chairs that have been welded together so they are too heavy to be picked up. I function in a world where there's a fine line between trust and deceit, and the slightest mistake can be fatal. I'm not afraid of anybody in my work environment, but nobody is above suspicion. At any given time, anybody can become a suspect, including employees. I guess working in a prison was never meant to be glamorous, but perhaps there is something sensual after all about the love-hate relationship one quickly develops during the adjustment period after arriving here. On the one hand, the inmates need all the despicable amenities prison life affords so they can survive. On the other hand, they really loathe themselves for not being able to choose something better. Let's face it, no one wants to voluntarily compromise their integrity, but when you have to choose between being sodomized so you can eat and being beaten nearly to death on a weekly basis, sodomy becomes less unattractive. The more you do it, the more it becomes a natural aspect of your everyday life. Unfortunately, the more time people spend behind bars indulging in raunchiness and the risqué, the more animalistic and inhumane they become. After several years in prison without support or contact from the outside world, most inmates finally become the heartless brutes people stereotype them to be.

I've worked here so long I've lost most of my sensitivity to rape, violence, theft, and murder. I don't condone it, but I stopped going home and asking God "Why?" years ago. I'm not a theological skeptic. I do believe in God the Father, Jesus Christ the Son, and the Holy Spirit, but I also believe there is something sinister coexisting in this world with us. How else can one explain the things people do to others and themselves? Our world has to be sick and demented for adults to have sex with children, for fathers to kill their own children to avoid paying child support, for women to kill other women over a man who wants neither of them, and for kids to beat other kids to death at school strictly for fun. As terrible as these crimes sound though, they are but small things compared to the crimes committed by the inmates housed in my prison. Even so, I treat these men like decent human beings without regard for why they are here. After years of working here and talking to hundreds of inmates, I have found that often times, the only thing standing between them and suicide or insanity is me. I don't have the power to change their situations, but being able to have a mature conversation with someone else who sees them as human sometimes gives them enough hope to live another day. I don't take that for granted. I've never been physically incarcerated, but I know what it's like to be socioeconomically bound by ideologies and theories that stifle your progress because you're a woman or a person of color. That being said, my job is fairly easy.

My alarm goes off at exactly 6:00 every morning, and the reality of being a female working in a prison sets in about 6:01. I rise, run or workout, shower, eat, and pray before I come to work. This is my lifestyle, and it hasn't changed in over ten years, not even when I'm on vacation. It sounds pretty mundane and it is, but I wouldn't change anything about it because I wouldn't be satisfied if I did. In fact, after all the years I've spent working behind bars, I don't think I could work in another environment. As crazy as that may sound, I actually enjoy doing what I do, and the challenges that come with teaching in a prison seem fairly normal to me compared to teaching in a public school. At least there's a reasonable excuse for violent behavior when a fight breaks out at a prison between inmates who have been excluded from society and housed in cages most of their lives. However, when a fight breaks out at a school and the kids have guns, knives, pipe bombs, and other weapons, there is no excuse. I feel sorry for the kids though, because public schools are becoming havens for kids with lazy, ignorant parents who aren't involved in their upbringing. These parents want and expect teachers to take on their parenting responsibilities at the expense of educating the students, which is the teacher's primary duty. Unfortunately, public school teachers have unreasonable demands placed upon them with very little support. That being the case, I'd rather be here teaching at a medium security level prison than in a public school. The only thing that really bothers me about working here is seeing so many young, talented, black men locked up. It's not just about crime or recidivism for those who are repeat offenders. It's something bigger that we are either overlooking or deliberately ignoring.

I have worked with inmates for many years, but I will never understand why any black male would deliberately do things that would cause him to be incarcerated for a prolonged period of time knowing if or when he is released, it will be more difficult for him to gain viable employment and reenter society than other ex-offenders. The mere thought of being controlled and having your freedom taken should be enough to make anyone think twice about committing crimes, but that is obviously not true. Furthermore, this cyclical issue creates an even bigger problem for black women because we are faced with the seemingly insurmountable task of trying to build a relationship with someone who is years behind us and, more than likely, who lacks formal education. It's a bitter pill to swallow for me to see these black men with so much potential functioning on the maturity level of junior high school students. Sadly, many of them are too immature to know or care about just how far behind they really are.

After spending ten or more years behind bars, the vast majority of them aren't marriage material, and they are so far behind the rest of the world that the woman has to stop moving forward in her own thing just to help him catch up to her past. There has been some meaningful dialogue about this issue before, but black women's opinions about the statistical nightmare they face are usually blanketed by some rhetoric from black men about slavery, the government and welfare, single parent homes, and the lack of support and patience on the part of black women. Black men are entitled to their own opinions, but the shifting of blame needs to stop because whether black women support them or not, they are overpopulating American prisons, and I see them every day.

Some of my black female friends have asked me over the years how I have managed to avoid dating an inmate. Naturally, they don't see what I see every day because they don't work in a prison. All they see are handsome men with sculpted bodies, tattoos, and a lot of attitude portrayed in films, which is not reality. Most of what they think about these men centers on lust and sexual fantasy. I always tell them though that the physical attraction will quickly dissipate the moment they sit down to have a meaningful conversation with these men. They think I'm being facetious when I tell them these men are functioning on a maturity level of someone half their age because they have never dated an inmate or ex-convict who has served a lot of time before. However, if they ever stopped daydreaming and took my advice to ask a woman who has tried dating an inmate, they would understand perfectly that separation is one of many obstacles they will face in that relationship, and the separation is not only physical.

Most of the women I have spoken to in support groups say that because you and the man are the same age, you have preconceived expectations, so you assume they know some of what you know and that they have accomplished some of what you have accomplished. You engage in verbal exchanges hoping to find some common interests, but you realize after they begin speaking that the two of you are really light years apart, and the man you are looking at is nothing more than a teenager wrapped up in an adult's body. You know he's at an obvious disadvantage because while you've been growing and achieving over the past twenty years, he has spent his time confined with and surrounded by other men who are just like him. You want to say something encouraging so you don't embarrass him or hurt his feelings, but you have to really craft your answers carefully because if you speak from your own experience level, he won't understand what you're saying. You can't really talk about things that are relevant to you at your age because owning a home and increasing the amount of money you contribute to your 401k are foreign subjects to him. You have to be honest and ask yourself if you can move forward with him. How much will it cost you to maintain a relationship with this man? How long will it take for him to catch up to you?

I have heard dozens of psychologists and other professional speculators say that one of the main reasons why black men, in particular, are incarcerated is because they don't have enough positive black male role models to live out loud what it means to be a good man. I believe there is some truth in that but only to a certain point. The lack of positive black male role models shouldn't be factored into every situation that involves a black male and a bad decision. The last time I checked, life was about choices; when you make bad ones, you still have to live with the consequences. God knows I've made my share of bad decisions, some of which I am still paying for today, but I didn't make all of those bad decisions because I didn't have a positive black female role model. I made some of those bad decisions because I was just being plain foolish. And if it's all about role models, then how do we explain prisoners who come from well-to-do families with college-educated, employed, Christian fathers who are actively involved in their upbringing? All inmates aren't poor, inner city, roguish kids from single-parent homes. Some of them are spoiled, suburban brats who need a few good whippings to curtail unwanted behavior.

Since we're on the subject of role models, I don't remember having a lot of positive black female role models during my formative years either. Other than the few black female teachers I had in elementary school and one or two women at church, few of the women I knew were college graduates. Most of them were homemakers who may or may not have made it out of high school. None of them were business owners or civic leaders, and none of them were engaged in anything that pertained to supporting or advancing women, especially black women. They were ordinary, everyday, black women who were naïve about global issues, stuffy and conservative because they were "saved," spent most of their time doing laundry and cooking, and did nothing spectacular that stood out and said, "Be like me." The most common denominators for all of them were marrying young, having kids early in life, and keeping the married woman's code of silence, even when they were beaten or cheated on by their husbands, to maintain the pretense of a happy marriage. They made a big to-do about being married, and they used the Bible as a weapon against women who wanted to leave their husbands when they were abused. In retrospect, I suppose they were role models — of everything I didn't want to be.

I come to work at this prison every day, and I look at all the black men here who have been seduced by the lie that suggests they aren't real men if they haven't spent time behind bars. Now that they are here, they find themselves in a courtship with a system that intends to marry them to a long incarceration sentence. They are intelligent and talented but wasted like good organs in a dead body. Sometimes I think they disgust me for being locked up because they didn't think about how their children were going to survive without a father or the struggle involved in raising them alone for the mother who is doing just that. I look at them and I feel sorry for all the black people who died during slavery and during the years of Jim Crow hoping freedom would be available for black people in the future. I watch them play cards and slap dominoes and tattoo new images of nonsense on their bodies, and I think about all the men — the real hard-working black men of the past — who managed to feed a family of possibly twelve or thirteen, buy land to leave an inheritance to their children, and pay to send their children to school without having the ability to read or write themselves. I wonder what those men would think if they were living today. I wonder how they would feel when they considered the price they paid with their lives for black men today to have the privilege of overpopulating the penal system.

I stand in front of the rail on the second-floor balcony and listen to the thunder of frustration and, eventually, rage in the obscenities they shout at anyone in earshot range. I see the despondency in their eyes, and they remind me of a bunch of thirteen-year-old and fourteen-year-old boys jousting with puberty, arguing over who committed a foul during that play on the basketball court, who got who's phone number at the dance, and who got "punked." They are like lost sheep who speak a color-coded language amongst themselves that only they understand, but their vernacular broadens, loses its color, and becomes inclusive when they are talking to non-black inmates or other inmates who are not in their clique. Although they publicly embarrass and verbally attack each other for show, there is a certain kind of distorted camaraderie they have that has invisible boundaries they don't cross with each other.

They wrestle with themselves and other men — black, white, or indifferent — attempting to function within an exclusive society of otherness that initially swallows them whole and then regurgitates them shortly after they arrive, but gradually submerges them in a modern institutional system of slavery as they develop their own sense of pseudo-comfort and trying to combine the socio-economic dysfunction and misplaced values they bring with them to their new environment. Some of them join gangs for protection and to feel some kind of connection to a brotherhood of men they think are similar to them. Some of them bury themselves in the library while taking all the classes the prison will allow them to take, so they can better themselves while keeping the reality of being in a 10 x 10 cage with another man from suffocating them and sifting their sanity like flour. Some of them become overwhelmed by the fear of being beaten and repeatedly raped by other men who prefer the rough hands, big feet, and Adam's apple of a man as an alternative to their imaginary women, so they acquiesce to their repugnance of homosexual relationships. Some of them just can't take it, and they do everything in their power to kill themselves or at least their sense of awareness, so the voices they hear that nobody else hears will stop calling them, and the hands they feel that nobody else feels will stop touching them.

I look at these men every day, and I want to tell them they've been lied to. There is no "the man" holding the key to black people's dreams and futures. This "the man" concept has functioned like a racial clothesline, which has allowed almost everybody who did something stupid or failed to do something they should've done to hang their garment of excuses and blame shifting there. I see these men and I want to tell them that battling the inequalities in American public education at an inner-city school in a crime-riddled neighborhood doesn't make you a criminal. Growing up in a single-parent home is not an automatic qualifier for prison, and you don't have to steal because there is an unequal distribution of wealth in this country either. Trying to persuade these men to accept this is extremely difficult, and I often get accused of being a sell-out because, according to them, I don't know the perils of being black in America anymore. Perhaps formal education and suburban living have changed me, but I'm not the self-righteous hypocrite they accuse me of being, and there is nothing wrong with moving away from low-income, high-crime neighborhoods to rear children in a safe environment with better opportunities. Even behind bars, some of these men aren't always willing to listen and accept responsibility for their actions, but it's not all their fault. The black community at large is just as much to blame as these men are because we have collectively excused them from responsibility by the double standards we perpetuate.

The double standard has crippled the black community by making provisions for black men to not be accountable at home, at church, and in our communities. It should not be acceptable for men to whore themselves with women or vices or to forsake their responsibilities, fiscally or in any other way, to their families. And since when did God not need black men to actively participate in church? If black women decided to leave black churches, they would cease to exist altogether. And the burden of a man's happiness, salvation, or success in this life does not rest on a woman's shoulders, although the double standard suggests this very thing. Women can't change men! If a man refuses to better himself, all the encouragement, support, and positive role models in the world doesn't matter — a point I try to instill in all of my students. Ultimately, the decision to change one's life can be influenced externally but must be settled and acted upon as a result of one's internal desire to be different.

I know there may be some residual effects of slavery involved in this cycle, but women and men alike still have to be accountable for their own actions. Bigotry, poverty, and the so-called inability of black women to teach young black males how to be men do not change the fact that, at the end of the day, life is still about choices. Regardless of whether you are poor, victimized by racism, or raised in a single-parent home, you still have to do the right thing. As lethal as this double-standard plague is to black people, it's not just a problem bearing down on the black community anymore. There are shiftless men of every race, and I have the curious privilege of teaching them English in this prison. I just hate to see that so many of them are black like me. It's almost like watching terminally ill people brought to a hospice to die.

CHAPTER TWO

I have often wondered why I committed myself to teaching English to a prison population filled with non-English-speaking residents, although all of my students were born in America.

I love teaching and I know it's really an escape for me because I get to travel to other places and be other people in the world of literature, but sometimes I think it's all vanity because I'm educating people, convicts rather, who are going to leave this prison one day only to have potential employers, lenders, and leasing agents. slam the door in their faces because they are ex-cons. If people in the free world are contributing to the recidivism problem in this country, does it really matter that a convict can read, write, and speak proper English when he leaves prison? What is an ex-con going to do with Shakespeare if he isn't allowed to reestablish himself as a working, law-abiding member of society? I know it's a crazy thing to think about, and I guess it's because I think about stuff like this that I keep coming back to the prison every day. Not to mention, listening to what the guys have to say about women is a real eye-opener sometimes.

I am one of the few female faces not in a prison uniform that these men get to see, so they, especially black inmates, like to use me as the national spokeswoman for all black women. I've been fortunate to establish a good rapport with the fellas, but they know where I stand on inappropriate relationships and personal propositions, so they don't cross that line with me. The first and most important rule in my class is respect. Because I emphasize this, my classroom is one of the few environments on this compound where the men can emotionally unveil themselves without worrying about who is going to spread what they said all over the prison. Consequently, on any given day, usually every day, they come to my class with questions or comments about something they heard or read involving women, in addition to their normal assignments. I know they feel comfortable talking to me about things they can't discuss with other inmates or prison staff members, so I respect their views of me as not just another woman but as someone they think can provide wise counsel, and I answer their questions in an educational way that forces them to see the reality of their statements. I try hard not to laugh at them as they search for words to frame what they want to say, but some of it is outrageously funny because it's usually something outlandish wrapped up in a male stereotype about women, and it's generally something about sex.

I find it so ironic at times that no matter how bad the conditions are in this prison, these guys talk about sex like women talk about hobbies, dieting, and their children, if they have any. They talk about it, read about it, dream about it, and write about it. More than half of the final compositions for my class last year were about sex or something sexually related. But for the men, sex is about identity and masculinity, not necessarily gratification. Women want gratification, and unless you're a prostitute, sex is an emotional and spiritual act, not just physical or financial. For these guys, sex is a rough, unromantic, social mechanism for them to exert some form of control over their environment. You can take everything away from them, but if they have at least one outlet to relieve some of the stress they live through daily, they have a better chance of surviving. Sex is an outlet that allows them to still feel human and connected to other humans, even though they are being excluded from humanity. Unfortunately, the only sexual partners they have are each other and the few lascivious prison guards who sleep with as many of them as will have him or her.

Aside from the gang fights, occasional riots, and random deaths that occur amongst the inmates, I can honestly say I am happy with my job. Some of my friends think I'm insane for working in a prison. Some of them also think I have become completely desensitized to all the things in life that are supposed to be considered beautiful and delicate and yadda, yadda, yadda, because I don't like flowers, candy, and stuffed animals. Well, I didn't like flowers, candy, and stuffed animals before I started working in the prison, but trying to persuade them is not really important to me, so I let them think they're right. Of course, being here is no walk in the park either. I still have to deal with male chauvinistic flippancy from time to time, especially the "disrespected black man" syndrome from one of the black prison guards in particular. If it's not him, then it's the black male chaplain who loves to tell me, "You're out of God's will for teaching male prisoners how to read, write, and speak English. You ought to be married and at home raising children." I don't treat him any differently from the way I treat the other chaplains, but he thinks that because he's an older black male I'm supposed to pay some additional homage to him and defer to him as my superior or my father. I just pray for the man and go on because apparently he's got some pride and self-esteem issues, but Sergeant Thomas takes the cake in disrespect and audacity.

Sergeant Baxter Thomas is one of the most revered guards at this prison. He commands respect from all the inmates and only the new ones are dumb enough to challenge him because they don't know what he's capable of. Is he dirty? You bet he is, and he will use whomever and whatever is at his disposal to maintain authoritative control of this prison. He's the perfect devil's advocate, which makes him ideal for this environment. In a sense, he is brilliant. On the other hand, Sergeant

Thomas is one of the biggest fools I know.

He likes to sleep with a lot of women, but he deliberately creates chaotic situations by sleeping with several women who all work at the same company, attend the same aerobics class, are related to each other, and so on. There is something about being divisive that appeals to him, and he works hard to divide people. I understand why he does it here at the prison, but why he chooses to use those same tactics in his personal life remains a mystery. Since the negative attention he draws to himself usually ends up following him here to work, he can't get promoted, although he is well equipped for the job. Of course, it is never his fault when bad things happen as a result of his conduct. According to him, he gets passed over for promotion because the board members are either racist or sexist, and he can't fathom why a woman with half a brain would possibly avoid him either. He interprets that as unfounded rejection, which is why I have to hear his mouth almost every day about why I won't go out with him. I get an ear full of, "You think you betta' than me 'cause you been to college" and "That's what's wrong with black women, y'all don't know how to respect black men" three or four times a week, and, of course, he makes sure he has audience when he says it. I just do what I normally do when he comes around: ignore him and leave. An ego as big as his is usually deflated when he finds himself talking to himself.

That being said, there are essentially seven major "social groups" or gangs in this prison: Los Serpientes (The Snakes, Hispanic), The Woods (short for "Pecker-Woods," white), Black Knights (black), She-males (homosexuals), Ecumenical Community (so-called Christians), Islamic Brotherhood (Muslims), and everyone else not affiliated with any of the aforementioned groups. All of the groups have a built-in code of treachery and allegiance they pledge to; it's how they survive behind bars. Even the Ecumenical Community has its own degree of hypocrisy it operates with because survival in here is based upon who outnumbers whom. It doesn't matter who you used to be before you got here; what matters is who you are or who you become after you arrive.

Naturally, the smallest group inside the prison is made up of the white males also known as Woods. They generally congregate amongst themselves except when their runners are doing business for them. Unlike the television images we're accustomed to seeing, the Woods aren't usually violent and overly aggressive unless they outnumber everyone else in that particular prison unit, which is rare for a state-operated facility. Most of the Woods are older, reclusive men who are serving long sentences, but there are some young white males as well who are not as antisocial as the older males. The older men from previous generations are trapped in the time zone they grew up in and have little exposure to new ideas, movements, changes, or progressions that have occurred since they became incarcerated. It's much harder for them to adapt to mingling with a mixed group of inmates because they were socialized and reared during a time when equality meant having people of color work as janitors and kitchen help for a company as opposed to having people of color as supervisors or division leaders. They don't really know how to approach non-white inmates because they've never been taught how to communicate with other non-white people and because they grew up with so many negative stereotypes of non-whites, especially non-white males. Many of them are really cowardly guys who have extreme and sometimes unfounded phobias about non-white males, so they move, eat, and play in packs like dogs. The younger males, however, have been exposed to and understand integrated cultures, so they have fewer reservations about hanging out with other non-white inmates.

The She-males is a male homosexual group that tries its best to function as both women and men in the prison. They try to carry themselves the way they assume real women would carry themselves: twisting when they walk, wearing make-up, crossing their legs when they sit down, and assembling their prison uniforms in ways that resemble women's clothing. The real man in them comes out though when they are threatened and backed into a corner. I have seen many She-males beat the crap out of other inmates who thought that just because they were gay, they couldn't fight. They might take hormones to alter their male features, wear high-heeled shoes, and smear lipstick across their lips surrounded by the remnants of a mustache and beard, but they are still biologically men. When their testosterone kicks in for self-preservation, they become nothing more than male killers in halter-tops and mascara.

As one might assume, they are housed in a separate wing for their protection because they are endangered species when they're alone in the general population. Many of the inmates despise them for being gay. It repulses them to think that a man with big rough hands, big rough feet, a heavy voice, and hair on his face, chest, and back would lie in bed with another man, who looks exactly the same, for sex. When they encounter She-males out in the open, the other inmates shun them and move away from them as quickly as possible because the She-males, although outnumbered, have no shame about openly recruiting new males they can "turn out" or expose to homosexuality. Sometimes open encounters can become violent when the targeted recruit is not interested in the She-male. However, if a host of She-males outnumber the recruits, they will attempt to rape them. If the She-males are successful, they will rape the recruits on a regular basis until the recruits lose their resistance and are completely converted. That may sound extreme, but there are other times, however, when a She-male will have an agreed domestic living arrangement with another man who is not supposed to be gay.

Some of the homosexuals in the prison are actual members of other gangs and not just She-males. When a gang has open or known homosexuals as members, they offer the She-males protection as long as they perform sexual acts for only the members of the gang or for a specific person in that gang. But they don't just have sex with the gang members. The She-males are also domestic partners who cook, clean, wash, iron, and perform other domestic responsibilities for the men they are involved with, so their arrangement is a simulation of a real relationship between a man and a woman who may actually live together. These relationships are the most dangerous kinds though, because the non-gay man involved in a closet relationship with a She-male may contract an STD or HIV from his She-male partner and pass that on to his girlfriend or wife when he is released or when he has a conjugal visit before his release.

The Ecumenical Community is a social group that is also housed in a separate wing in the prison. They are mostly white males, with a few other non-white males too, and are non-violent and standoffish. They aren't necessarily cowards, but their religious conviction keeps them from being aggressive or retaliating against other inmates unnecessarily. They will fight if it's absolutely unavoidable, but mostly they try to maintain some level of peace through perceived diplomacy. Their wing is usually quiet, and most of the inmates have their own hobbies they participate in without pressure to be uniformed like a gang. The only drawback to it is that the Ecumenical Community is comprised mostly of white males who, after all these centuries, still try to use the Bible to unjustly scrutinize the other non-white inmates in the wing. The worst part of the whole ordeal is that they do it with an even tone of voice and a smile. It's not an easy pill to swallow when someone tells you that you're inferior to him or her because of the color of your skin in the name of Jesus, but somehow the non-white inmates find ways to overlook their stupidity and coexist peacefully on that wing.

The Islamic Brotherhood is the total opposite of the Ecumenical Community. The group is mostly dominated by black inmates who are members of the Black Knights gang. Their primary reason for associating themselves with Islam to begin with is because most Muslims aren't white, and there are no pictures of a blond-haired, blue-eyed Jesus that they don't relate to. It is a religion that appeals to downtrodden, overlooked, and impoverished people. It's not about loving God and really wanting to bring positive change into the world or even the prison for that matter. Their brand of Islam is about forming a brotherhood of inmates who want to be avenged of the powers that be because they believe they are being systematically eliminated from the pool of potential prospects for a happy life. When I look around every day and see all the black inmate faces in this prison, I sometimes think that they aren't too far off the mark with what they believe.

The Black Knights is an all-black prison gang with veins in prisons that expand over more than half the country. They are violent and involved in anything criminal you can imagine, which also means they are well paid and influential. When black inmates first arrive, the Black Knights send an emissary to meet them at their cell doors with an ultimatum: join or die. It's as simple as that because they know the prison is ultimately controlled by whichever gang has the most members. The new converts are cloistered like monks so they can be trained in gang hierarchy and protocol. After the new recruits have gone through their initial training, they have to commit some kind of crime to begin earning rank within the gang. That's when things really get ugly because the recruits are usually sent on dangerous missions like kamikazes to take out notorious archrivals of the gang that other gang members couldn't kill. Like confused chickens, the new recruits cluck along at the gang leader's bidding trying to pull off a nearly impossible crime. Most of the new recruits end up dead or severely wounded.

Los Serpientes is the largest Hispanic gang in North America, with contacts in every prison across the country and ties to the Mexican and Columbian drug cartels. It is the most diabolical gang ever known to mankind. The gangs and crime organizations of the early twentieth century couldn't hold a candle to Los Serpientes. Of course, its main source of income is drugs: cocaine, heroin, and marijuana. The gang also ships inestimable amounts of high-powered weapons into the country, which are usually discovered at the scene of a major crime involving drugs. Since it is the most vicious gang in the prison system, the members don't always do things in packs, and they don't always respect the other gangs in the prison either. It really depends on whether they overpopulate that particular unit or not. When they do have the run of a unit, they control it from the inside out and use it as a host to import their drugs and weapons through elaborate communication lines, intimidation, and a lot of carefully planned bribery.

Aside from their illegal activities, they are noted mostly for their cruelty. Los Serpientes members have a tendency to torture their victims before they kill them. The torture alone is not surprising, considering the fact that they are connected to drug cartels that do the same thing. The incredulous part is how they torment their victims. When you find a body that has been tortured by the Los Serpientes, it might have poked-out eyeballs, severed genitals, body parts cut off and sewn back on the body in the wrong place, or missing internal organs. You never know what you are subject to find with them.

Nevertheless, my unit has somewhat of a balance of power because there are just as many Black Knights here as there are Los Serpientes, and they both use the Woods and the She-males as minions to do their dirty work whenever they can. No matter how much crime the gangs are involved in or what kind of beef they have with each other, I don't allow them to disrupt my class with their issues. My classroom is part of a neutral zone where the playing field is leveled for everyone. Notwithstanding, I also keep a gun in my classroom.

In addition to my teaching duties at the prison, I am a member of the review board that oversees paroles, transfers, legal hearings, and other issues related to inmate placement. I am also a member of an in-house committee that investigates crimes in special categories. These crimes were categorized as such because they didn't really exist in America until our economy bottomed out. They all had some degree of evil behind them, but the people who committed the crimes weren't all prison inmates. Still, we were tasked to work with local law enforcement and Border Patrol agents to gather as much information as possible so we could try to reestablish some ethical mediums in our society, which seemed almost impossible given the current state of affairs in the country. Nonetheless, the job was interesting, to say the least, and required a cast-iron stomach and open mind because anything that could happen usually did.

Just last week, I sat in on one of the investigation interviews with the local police who captured a woman boiling a child. When they asked her why she did it, she did not respond. She simply gazed at them as if she had relocated to another dimension of reality years ago, and they were intruding on her right to live there. She made no effort to defend herself, and since she was caught in the act, they were determined to send her to prison. When they brought the confession statement out for her to sign, she laughed and mocked them and psychologically withdrew herself from the current moment to go back into the state of reality that was real to her. One of the officers rose to cuff the woman's hands behind her back but he jumped suddenly after he reached into the long sleeves of the dirty brown coat she was wearing. When he raised her sleeves, we were all stunned to see that this woman had eaten her own hands off. Nevertheless, we all knew she was homeless and starving, so there was no need to ask why. Under normal conditions, this woman would've been taken to a psychiatric unit for treatment. However, most of the mental asylums were closed due to lack of funding, so the criminally sane and mentally disturbed served time together. Sadly, incidents like these were becoming common.

One of the other major issues we dealt with had to do with determining appropriate sentences for these special issues because some of the things that were happening weren't actually illegal, but they were unethical. For example, millions of elderly people in our society were already receiving checks from their pension plans and social security, but they had significant health problems and needed nursing assistants to come to their homes and help them. Unfortunately, things were so bad economically, nobody could be trusted, especially if the elderly person was bed-ridden. The nursing assistants, nursing home staff, neighbors, or their adult children would steal from them while they watched helplessly from their beds, the floor, or wherever they were left. They were tired of being taken advantage of and decided that mobility was the only way they could take care of themselves until they died.

They began forming groups with seniors who were still mobile and devised a way to gain mobility back for themselves. We found some of their solicitations in newspapers and other periodicals that were still in circulation. They made arrangements to barter with the healthy poor in exchange for the body part or parts they needed to become mobile. Since this was all done voluntarily and the body parts weren't stolen or previously assigned to some donor list, it wasn't technically illegal. I personally didn't like handling cases in this category because I empathized with the seniors; the government didn't like it because they said it made Americans look too primitive, but I suppose cannibalism and eating off your hands didn't.

Be that as it may, I usually arrive to work about two hours before my first class begins because I always have students waiting outside my classroom door to see me, but it's not always about school work. A lot of the inmates don't trust the prison staff members, including the chaplains, because they've either heard about something they did that violated their rights as inmates or they've experienced it firsthand. Today, one of my students came to see me about something he heard and had kind of pieced together with whatever Spanish he learned hanging around Spanish-speaking inmates. He said the Hispanic inmates — gang members actually — had some outside connections that were going kill some politicians and other important people in American society as payback for exploiting Hispanic workers and residents in general. It was supposed to be a mass movement that was organized and funded through some kind of underground Hispanic society.

Now I knew there was a lot of political talk about this and that as it pertained to the swelling population of illegal residents in America. These talks had been going on for years, and some of the border-states had actually created laws that profiled Hispanics for possible deportation. When my student Bizz — a nickname given to him because he always knew everybody's business — told me this, I didn't completely dismiss the idea, but I didn't sound any alarms just yet either. I didn't have enough evidence to call a meeting with the committee members. All I had to go on was the word of an inmate, which may or may not have been true. To be on the safe side, I taped the conversation and wrote down everything he said and the date he came to me so I could refer to it if indeed something happened as he described. I put the paper in my office safe, sat down behind my desk with my back toward the door, and prayed silently in my office. When I finished praying, I decided to call my father to inquire about what was going on in the world of politics. I worked too much to really know what was going on in the world outside these walls. My father, however, kept up with all the latest news and could tell you about whatever was happening in America or abroad on any given day.

My father said there was supposed to be a major political announcement made in a press conference in two days. I asked him what the announcement was about. He said he believed some folks from Congress intended to introduce some more corrupt legislation designed to alienate Hispanics based on some unrealistic statistics some of the southern politicians invented to force the government's hand on immigration policies. I had a feeling that something bad was going to happen because every time southern politicians ganged together in the past, something bad usually did happen. I had always been fond of quiet country living, so I made it a point to keep property in sparsely populated rural places. I urged my family to take shelter in my country hideout just outside of the county to avoid the possible turmoil that was going to erupt from this announcement. The place was tucked away in the woods and was not visible from the main road. It was good that they listened because the day the announcement hit the airwaves, millions of citizens from numerous cities, counties, and states in the south and other places with large Spanish-speaking populations protested with a vigorous feeling of betrayal that was only bolstered by other public announcements, no less important, from CEOs and city, county, and state officials who were equally involved in the scandal.

The announcement to profile Hispanics literally took us back to a point of racial division that was like segregation during the era of Jim Crow. No one imagined these politicians would have the audacity in the twenty-first century to bring back these kinds of laws, and people everywhere were livid. Black faces, white faces, Spanish faces, and other faces took to the streets, enraged by their disdain for corrupt politicians. Fires, looting, desecration, and deliberate acts of violence chased street corners in many communities and were committed by anyone who believed he or she was being victimized by political treachery. Smoke darkened the skies over various segments of the country while the fiendish politicians who orchestrated this mess tried to go underground to run from the monster they created. There was no such thing as a safe place to hide in the city or the suburbs anymore, although some of the homeless tried to hide in sewers and in dumpsters to avoid the commotion caused by the riot. The President declared a national state of emergency and tried to muster up troops to police the cities under martial law, but some of the National Guard soldiers refused to stand against the angry mobs because they were still infuriated about the fact that they had lost so many comrades in the Middle East for nothing more than political self-indulgence and oil supplies that America never could control.

People were running and screaming at the tops of their lungs, holding hatchets, knives, guns, and anything else that could be used as weapons. Babies were crying in their mothers' arms while they scurried along with the crowds to participate in the destruction. Helicopters were circling over various parts of the country, but there was nothing they could do from the sky but watch and film the activity for people like me, who were trapped inside a building working in a position that could not be abandoned. Some people hurriedly left their jobs and sped across bridges and highways trying to escape, but disaster caught them in midday rush hour traffic, and they became hostages to angry masses who were armed with about as much hatred as a beguiled nation could be. Fire trucks were trying to drive past people in the streets, but the crowds were so dense that they crept along a few feet at a time. Even so, the fires were too numerous to attempt putting them all out. Some people hung over the balconies of high-rise apartment buildings and screamed at the folks in the street, only to have rocks and shoes thrown at them. And the children, the poor children, were everywhere: on playgrounds at school, at home sick, at the doctor's office with their parents getting mandatory vaccinations, on sidewalks, and in the streets. They had no idea what was happening. They just realized they were in the middle of it, and their Sunday school teachers, neighbors, best friends' dads, and football coaches were all involved.

Trampled here, trampled there, bodies were stacking up everywhere. Nobody stopped running and screaming long enough to see whom the dead were. They just stepped over them and kept going. Day after day, more and more people looted and burned what they didn't get to the day before. After a few days, the flesh-eating birds came to feed upon the carcasses that covered the sidewalks and streets and fields where humans fell dead. There were so many birds that the smoke-filled skies were overtaken by them like millions of small planes trying to land at one airport at the same time; they hovered in the sky until they selected the body they wanted. Mice, roaches, and flies were summoned by the stench of dead humans and mildewed food from looted grocery stores that was carried about by winds blowing in all directions. For once, I was truly glad to be in that prison, for I dared to think but was convinced I might have easily participated in the protests had I been on the streets when the announcement was made.

No one born in the twenty-first century had ever seen disaster and wretchedness to this degree. Not even the Civil Rights Movement protests were this bad. We were warned about the possibilities because of the initial outrage behind legalized ethnic profiling with Hispanics, but we didn't really think it would happen in our lifetimes. I suppose if anyone wanted to compare it to something historically familiar, they might say that looking at some of the southern parts of America now was like looking at America during the period of Reconstruction after the Civil War. Nonetheless, many of us prepared ourselves for the worse, but some people thought it was all a political ploy by whoever wanted to be elected next, which really didn't matter anymore because the damage was irreversible.

Meanwhile, the government was finally forced to focus on domestic poverty and other issues that ate away at the American resources that were left, which means we retracted a great deal of the international aid we had given to other countries. Our immigration borders were finally closed because the deteriorating middle-class sector of our economy couldn't afford to carry the weight of the country anymore, and the cost of rebuilding the country after the riots would financially strangle what middle class we had left. After we closed our borders, the government made sweeping reforms to the welfare and low-income housing system, which really had no effect on the poor. The shrinking middle class and the wealthy were hit the hardest. The reforms and other hard political decisions were necessary evils America had to adopt to rebuild and keep it afloat. Regrettably, poverty was becoming as prevalent in America as HIV is in Africa, but there wasn't a single factor that could be isolated to reverse it, although some economic strategists projected our financial wounds would be mysteriously healed by the invisible hands of time. There may be some truth in that, but time, so far, hasn't allowed us to forget the wrongs we have committed against others and ourselves, and if people who existed before our time were given a chance to view us now, they would collectively agree that this was a time of reckoning. All the years of cutthroat, manipulative diplomacy had come back to bite us in our behinds, and we were forced to bargain with countries we previously labeled "third world."

The destruction of the American south left little unharmed. Actually, only about one-fourth of the south was truly ravished, but the American economy was already strained before the riots so the damage seemed worse than it really was. Politicians were hidden by what fraction of government was left, but some of them were found and slaughtered in the streets. The mere fact that they were killed was not surprising though. On the contrary, the most shocking thing about their murders was how they were killed. As an employee in a prison, I have seen many dead bodies disfigured, burned, beheaded, and in some cases mutilated, but nothing compared to the acts of carnage committed against American politicians. Some diabolical group had to cooperatively agree to do these things because one person couldn't have killed them all this way. Some Good Samaritans here and there decided to secure the bodies, or what was left of them, when the violence began to settle so they could help the families give these politicians some kind of decent burial and lay them to rest because all of them weren't guilty. The Samaritans were only trying to help, but this was a hard thing, not just for the victims' families but for all of us, because the only parts of their bodies that remained were their heads, arms and hands, and legs and feet. The torsos had been taken and never recovered.

The pictures were sent to every prison in the nation so the Special Crimes Committees could see them to determine whether the butchery bore a resemblance to someone inside who may have residual gang members on the streets or if this was something entirely new. Based on the information we had available, this wasn't something new, but it wasn't from somebody inside that we knew about, at least not at that point in time. Our research indicated this type of killing was in fact antiquated and may have originated in the Americas before the European settlers arrived, which baffled us because expertise in ancient cultures that practiced this type of ritual slaughter would've been limited to archaeologists and anthropologists. As far as we knew, there were no groups of violent archaeologists in the country, so we put the pictures in a private file and kept quiet about them until we gathered more information from cultural experts that were called in to interpret them.

I remembered the conversation I had with Bizz before all the excitement began, so I had him brought to my office to reopen the issue we previously discussed. I showed him one of the pictures and asked him what he knew about the killing style. He said the Hispanic inmates told him that the practice of taking a human torso comes from some old tribal ritual carried out by "Los Antiguos," or the Ancients. I believed Bizz was telling me the truth about what he knew. He didn't have anything to gain from ratting out the Hispanic gang members, and even though he was a Mexican-American, he couldn't speak a lick of Spanish, so he couldn't have made up such an elaborate story on his own. I didn't want other inmates to see Bizz spending an excessive amount of time in my office and assume he was snitching or having an inappropriate relationship with me, so I gave him a pass to spend the rest of his afternoon in the library reading: a common task generally assigned to my students.

I was never fond of the practice of using inmates against other inmates because it just seemed so dishonest to me. People who are motivated by greed will say and do anything for a little comfort in a prison. Besides, inmates don't snitch on each other because they believe in right or wrong necessarily. They do it because they are being threatened and need protection, they want to reduce their sentence, or because they hate the other person. Bizz, on the other hand, was an unusual inmate who really didn't have close ties to any clique in particular. He was smart enough to associate with everybody so he could know what was going on, but he kept enough distance from people to avoid being considered a threat. Out of all the fights or riots that have ever occurred at this prison, Bizz has never been implicated in any of them, which is a testimony all by itself. He only had about three or four years of his sentence left, which really meant a year to two years in actual time, so the need to reduce his sentence wasn't a motivating factor. I made some inconspicuous inquiries about him to some of the guards and other inmates for safety reasons because trust is not something you give away in an environment like this. You have to know whom you're dealing with. A mistake could lead to an untimely death, including your own. According to them, he was an average inmate who functioned under the radar. If he had connections or specific skills that would contribute to any of the gangs' purposes, nobody knew about it. Everybody thought he was safe.

By and by, he came to me with new information about the killings and about some of the staged riots that took place in the prison. I started doing my own research so I could compile some information to present to the committee when the time was right. I discovered some very interesting facts about Los Antiguos. Legend has it that there were essentially three main tribes in the Americas before the arrival of Europeans who believed in a mythical place called the Underworld. There were three councils comprised of six Lords in the Underworld. Likewise, the Ancients or Los Antiguos was a council of tribal elders comprised of six men for each of the three tribes. These elders were proven bloodthirsty warriors who were selected to their tribal councils because of their violence and wickedness. Supposedly, the council legislated policies that were given to them by the Lords of the Underworld to govern the three tribes. According to the legend, every eighteen years, a member of the council had to render the ultimate sacrifice in order to join the Lords of the Underworld. This also meant a new member was chosen to join Los Antiguos. From what I read, the competition was fierce because Los Antiguos were regarded as the highest authorities on earth. Therefore, whoever was chosen had to be more diabolical than his other competitors, which ultimately meant the sacrifices they offered had to exceed what we would normally characterize as perverse.

Instantly, images of human carnage came to my mind as it raced through hundreds of thousands of memories trying to recall something it could relate to what I just read. For a few minutes, I was actually overcome by curiosity and a little fear of the unknown. Sacrificing or stealing human torsos had never been documented in this country, to my knowledge. An entire list of random yet logical questions came forward such as, "What is significant about a human torso?", "What object could be used to butcher a torso?", "Who would have the stomach to do it?", and "Why would they do it now?" I couldn't fathom having something or somebody like this in our society today. Torture and murder happens in the prison daily and I have seen some of the most gruesome killings ever documented, but the mere idea of human sacrifice becoming a common or accepted practice in the twenty-first century is mind-boggling. I sat there for a moment, contemplating different ways to approach the subject with the committee members who are so skeptical about everything that can't be proven scientifically. I put all the documents I had gathered and the notes I took from Bizz in a folder in my safe and left my office for some fresh air.

CHAPTER THREE

I had been calling my father at least three times a week to make sure he and my mother were doing well and to get an update on what was happening outside the prison. I had a cellar in the house filled with canned goods and a nice stock of wine, and I also had a cellar in the bottom of the shed behind the house loaded with additional supplies and toiletries if they needed them. I made sure the house was always stocked because I only went out to that country hideaway once every other month when I wasn't working overtime, grading papers, or dealing with a new case on the committee. My father had been watching the footage on the news about the riots since they began a few weeks ago. When I spoke to him a few days ago, he said things were slowing down and people were getting tired of destroying things. He predicted everything would come to an end in just a few days because it took too much energy for people to maintain that kind of anger and to keep demolishing things.

"Once you've drained all your energy trashing all the stuff around you, you start coming to your senses because something called 'self-preservation' kicks in, and you realize that most of what you need to survive is now gone," my dad said. "If you destroy whatever is left, you'll die."

My dad is a very intelligent but simple man filled with wisdom and what he predicted came true.

When I called him this afternoon, he said that suddenly, out of nowhere but perhaps triggered by a whole lot of providential intervention and the smallest drops of human civility, Americans stopped killing, looting, fighting, and protesting. Everything just stopped like an invisible cloth of satisfaction was blanketing the earth. After the blazing cinders and charred remains of everything began to settle and die out, the site of decaying human bodies and dilapidated buildings caused people to begin psychologically collecting themselves, and they just stopped like there were silent voices in the atmosphere sending them subliminal messages. It seemed as if they finally realized that after everything was destroyed, they still had to live so there was no point in fighting anymore. They had done all they could do to express their anger and disgust, and their voices were indeed heard. So when everybody stopped and the chaos was truly over, the President and some other politicians called for a massive clean-up, and people started filing in lines here and there like worker ants to volunteer their services. It was almost as if the riots hadn't just happened, but we know they did because the cities and towns were left looking like a massive tornado had just leveled them.

These were undoubtedly hard times and rebuilding was going to take something we already lacked: money. Little by little, however, communities were coming back together and people — blacks, whites, Asians, and others — were laying down their prejudices so we could live. Unfortunately, the exception to this utopian experience was still Hispanics. Despite all the shady deportation efforts though, the Hispanic population in America continued to grow almost exponentially. In fact, it was growing so fast that all of the border-states in America were riddled with an abundance of Hispanic ghettos in every part of the state, a triumph credited to a movement they called, "La Raza," which means, the Race.

I heard about this so-called movement to reclaim the southern states for Mexico several years before the riots here in America. Nobody really believed Hispanics would take over the United States. Honestly speaking, nobody believes it now either. Sure, there are tens of millions of them in this country, but the vast majority of them are poor and undereducated, and many of them can't speak English. Even if they did take the southern part of the United States back and claim it for themselves or for Mexico, they don't have the money or technology to do anything with it. Perhaps the Europeans felt that way too when they came to claim land for their kings and queens. I suppose they saw America as an undeveloped goldmine, but the natives were standing in their way.

Regardless, it is not hard to believe they would conceive such an idea. They have felt indignant for many centuries about losing land to whites who migrated west from Europe and colonized the Americas. They want the land they lost to the United States back, and they believe America owes them something for it. I can't say I really blame them for feeling that way. I understand what it's like to have other people take from you, but I don't dwell on the historical mistakes that were made in this country because at least black people are better off now in America than they would've been if they remained in some of the third-world countries that sold African slaves to Europeans. Hispanics, however, are not quite as forgiving, and they have been holding centuries-long grudges. Some Hispanic groups hate Americans because of our lavish lifestyles, but most of their hatred and sense of entitlement toward America exists because their governments' corruption and greed force its own citizens to starve to death.

Mexico and most Central American countries don't really have a middle class to carry the economic weight of their nation, so the rich grow richer while the poor continue to be malnourished under the most inhumane conditions the world has ever seen next to those in Africa. They also feel powerless against their own governments because they often recruit drug cartels and dirty police officers to execute any person, group, or faction who dares to speak against them. People protest in these countries, but their country constitution doesn't make provisions for true democracy. Therefore, they are left to choose between starving in their own countries and becoming a member of the new slave labor class in America. Many of them have chosen to join America's slave labor class, which is systematically controlled by politicians and business expansionists who exploit Hispanic workers to avoid the cost of paying American workers. The new undocumented workers can live a better life in America earning minimum wage, living in government subsidized housing, and receiving federally funded benefits, including healthcare, which is better for them and their families in the long run. However, politicians and business expansionists made the mistake of thinking Hispanics would continue to allow American businesses to exploit them. They assumed that once the illegal aliens got here, they would be quiet and passively agree with politicians who left the immigration door open because, quite frankly, the politicians and expansionists were doing them a favor by allowing them to live in America and reap the benefits of federal social programs they didn't pay for, but they were wrong.

Before the American south was reduced to rubble, Hispanics across the United States started forming committees and mass protest demonstrations demanding civil rights and other things because they were beginning to outnumber us. I thought it was somewhat odd because they weren't all citizens, and I never knew that illegal aliens could demand things like civil rights from host countries. Howbeit, they started scheduling marches across different parts of the country, but the government wasn't sure about how they needed to address it. According to our constitution, they weren't entitled to receive some things because they didn't have citizenship so there was only so much we could give them, but even if we could meet their demands, it wasn't fair to the citizens, and some of their demands were unreasonable anyway. For example, they started demanding wages that people who had college degrees earn and access to establish businesses in gated communities where the financial elite lived. When the wealthy refused to patronize their businesses, they said it was discrimination. Next, they demanded tax breaks and reparations for losses they claimed resulted from the Spanish-American War. When the government failed to acquiesce, they picketed their jobs and refused to work because they knew that the livelihood of most businesses was based upon their willingness to perform unskilled labor at low wage rates. Some of the more liberal politicians tried to create legislation that would benefit citizens and immigrants alike, but the conservatives wouldn't have it. When they found a loophole they could use under "states' rights," they concocted some more prejudiced legislation that led to a smaller civil war.

After America was destroyed behind the scandal and our borders were officially closed, the majority of American citizens voted to have all the illegal Hispanic residents and their children removed as quickly as possible before violence against them erupted, but they refused to leave and pledged for the sake of "La Raza" that they would fight to the death. The government started deporting them, but there were far too many of them to purge America. Aside from this, some of the Hispanic-American citizens hid illegal aliens in various places across the United States like the Underground Railroad during the days of slavery. The aliens who lived out in the open formed their own self-appointed militia patrols to guard their neighborhoods against anyone who was not Hispanic, but they also made a pact or treaty of some kind amongst themselves to destroy the southern part of the United States if they couldn't take it by force. I found out a great deal about what they were planning to do because the Hispanic gangs at my prison would pass out flyers to stage riots the same time these militias protested and raided throughout the southern half of the nation. We knew the gangs were rioting and keeping up ruckus inside the prison to show some solidarity for their Hispanic brothers and sisters outside the prison, but it never occurred to me or anyone else on the committee that the gangs at my prison were a part of some other massive underground movement, especially one dedicated to targeting politicians.

We started watching the movements of Hispanic gangs in the prison after we found one of their flyers about rioting. There were also obscure instructions on how they needed to unify and mobilize Hispanic inmates across the United States to overtake American prisons on these leaflets, which is what disturbed us most. We couldn't make out all of what the leaflets said because part of it was written in Spanish and another part was coded with gang symbols they made up themselves. We were able to determine that they were enraged because the government refused to listen to the demands of free Hispanics who were protesting in the streets, so they figured the government would definitely respond to armed Hispanic inmates with American hostages. Quite naturally, there is no honor among inmates, and you will always have snitches that are willing to give information in exchange for privileges or a reduced sentence. After the flyers began circulating, that very thing happened. A snitch came to members of the Special Crimes Committee with information about a stabbing that would be used to stage a prison riot. It came as no surprise to us to find out that the gang responsible for the stabbing was going to be Los Serpientes, or the Snakes.

The gang at my prison, called Los Serpientes, was the largest Hispanic prison gang in America, and there was only one way to get in: murder. Murder of any kind and of anybody would grant an inmate an interview with one of the viceroys of the gang leader, Cobra. Los

Serpientes were notorious for brutality and they usually killed in packs. Now there were several other gangs in the prison system. However, Los Serpientes held a league of their own because of the reputation they had for the use of prolonged torture. They were the only known gang to torment their victims for hours before they killed them.

Last year, we found one of their victims in a storeroom the prison used to keep extra mattresses and bedding in. They had already beaten this inmate to death before they rolled his body in salt, but that wasn't the worst part of it. Before they beat the man, they forced him to crawl on his hands and knees on a floor covered with thumbtacks. Afterwards, they broke all the man's fingers with pliers and cut his toes off with handmade box cutters. When they finished, they stripped him naked and beat him with pillowcases filled with broken glass and nails. By the time they rolled his battered body in salt, he was already dead, but this one of the Los Serpientes' milder cases. We figured the assailants were probably new members of the gang who were trying to impress the viceroys because older gang members usually disfigured their victims so bad, they wouldn't be identifiable without dental records. Los Serpientes made it a point to leave a few teeth, so we could identify the body, and they could intimidate the rest of the prison population. When other inmates found out who the deceased was, it usually kept things quiet for a little while because Los Serpientes didn't target weaklings.

The snitch came to us and told us he would voluntarily give us information in exchange for protection, of course, which meant isolation from the general population, and a few extra privileges none of us found objectionable. He requested several notepads, pencils, a map of the country, and a little privacy so he could decipher the letters that were circulating in the prison. He knew what the symbols meant because he used to be a runner in what the inmates call "the neutral zone." The neutral zone is an imaginary zone that exists where runners or emissaries from each gang meet to do business with each other. The runners are usually marked by special tattoos or symbols painted on their faces or necks, and they are one of few inmates who have access to things that inmates generally can't get without help outside the prison walls and money to bribe the guards. Runners are the greatest assets to any gang, but they can also be the gangs' worst enemies because they know everything — legal and illegal — the gang is doing, and it all passes through them.

The snitch was given an unusual nickname by Los Serpientes. They called him "Dios," which literally means god, but in a different sense than what most people are accustoming to hearing. Los Serpientes never capitalized his name because they thought it was blasphemy since they were mostly Catholics, but they gave him this title because he was an iconic figure whose access to everything merited him a certain kind of preeminence over other inmates. Nonetheless, he came to us to exact revenge upon Los Serpientes because they replaced him with another gang runner after they suspected he was stealing money out of their profits. In addition, it was good for him because he was no longer protected but was instead a target of opposition. All the inmates knew runners were usually killed after they lost their usefulness because they knew too much, so Dios could be attacked at any moment.

After three or four days, he brought us a stack of papers and some drawings from one of the prison tattoo artist. We already knew what the Spanish writing meant, but he went on to educate us about the gang symbols and tattoos, which were drawn by an inmate tattoo artist called "The Scribe." Each symbol represented a topographical feature on the map or other random location, which is how they were communicating riot locations to each other without being explicit in their flyers. The Scribe, who drew the symbols on the flyers, tattooed symbols on inmates' bodies because it enabled them to disseminate information in the prison at a much faster rate. According to Dios, when they needed to make sudden changes to their plans, the Scribe would draw another symbol that overlapped the first one with new instructions. When Spanish-speaking inmates saw it, they knew exactly what to do and where to go. If somebody stopped to ask them what was going on, they had a coded answer, gang symbol, or tattoo that only they understood. Also, they changed scribes every so many years to alter the style of the symbols and tattoos they were using, which made it even more difficult for us to unscramble their messages. As we began to understand the magnitude of what was happening behind these walls, we thought it best to contact the FBI and plant undercover officers in the general population.

When the FBI agents first arrived, they assembled a small group of officers and the entire committee to brief us on the intelligence they already had about Los Serpientes. They told us then they had been watching some of their outside contacts for a while because they had connections to affluent Hispanic cartel members who were supplying most of the drugs inside the prisons and on the streets of America, but more importantly, the peculiar style of their killings troubled the government and law enforcement because the tactics were unheard of. They showed us several pictures of their victims' remains that were discovered, and they told us things about the leader, Cobra, which left us awestruck. When we saw the pictures, we all mutually agreed that Los Serpientes had to be connected to the brutal murders of the politicians who were killed during the riots because some of their victims' torsos were missing. At that time, we thought it necessary to bring in Dr. Leonardo Vinson: the new staff anthropologist, who was hired to educate us about the ancient cultures of North and South American civilization before colonization.

Dr. Vinson was a short man with white hair and an ever-serious look on his face even when he was joking. He wore wire-rim glasses, usually on the tip of his nose, plaid sweaters, blazers, and bowties, all typical clothing one would expect an anthropologist or a man of his academic standing to wear. Nevertheless, he was a very pleasant man who excited and intrigued us every morning in the break room when he recounted details of his experiences and many travels while we waited for the coffee to finish brewing. Aside from the volumes of books he published, the international scientific accolades he received, and the notable research excursions he spearheaded, he was a fun-loving grandfather who spent hours investing in his grandson's scientific curiosities and teaching him how to fish.

Dr. Vinson had been working on a slide show about ancient culture that he was going to use for his presentation to us. He only had a few of the pictures that were distributed throughout the prisons, but after he saw the pictures from the FBI, he told us that it was urgent he show us his presentation right then because the FBI's pictures supported his theories about ancient ritual killing and the deaths of the politicians. Immediately, we helped him gather his books and charts and made quick copies of his documents for the presentation; we were all quite interested in knowing how these things were connected and what, if anything, we could do to stop them. All twelve members of the committee and the FBI agents were scurrying along moving this and setting up that in anxious anticipation of what Dr. Vinson was going to say. After thirty minutes or so of fast-paced shuffling, we were finally ready. We turned off all the lights, closed the blinds, and sat in dead silence, sipping coffee or water and watching the blank screen until Dr. Vinson's slideshow came into focus on the projector.

So we could understand fully where he was going, he gave us a brief historical overview about different tribes on the northern and southern American continents that were prominent but also susceptible to violence, which was understandable to a point considering the material wealth these tribes possessed. Naturally, both trust and loyalty were of the essence to keep kingdoms of this magnitude functioning smoothly. Primarily, there were three tribes that controlled all the other smaller tribes on the continents, and they all believed in sacrificing humans to the idols they worshipped. Dr. Vinson told us the natives of these tribes believed in a legend about a doorway or portal to hell that allowed supernatural beings or, for lack of a better word, spirits, who served as ambassadors to their gods to pass through. If the spirits took an evil report back to their gods, humans would be punished by various means including famine, hurricanes, earthquakes, and other natural disasters. The only way to pacify these idols was to offer them a blood sacrifice, but it had to be human blood because, according to the idols, humans were committing the offenses, not animals.

As Dr. Vinson continued, he showed us pictures of possible prehistoric tools used to mutilate humans and the killing grounds where humans were hung upside down to be drained of their blood after they were killed. Last, he told us about a legend of a tribal chieftain who was enthroned centuries before the Americas were discovered. He said this tribal leader was completely enthralled with the act of mutilating humans, so much that it became a daily practice during his reign. No one was exempt from his terror, not even his family. After a few years that he had been king, some of his council leaders conspired to have him removed from the throne because they believed he was a bedlamite. When this chieftain found out about the plot, he summoned every witchcraft worker, shaman, soothsayer, and magician that could be found and paid them to call up as many evil spirits as possible to endow him with the ultimate powers of darkness so he could rid himself of the traitors in his kingdom.

According to the legend, after the ceremony was performed, this king assembled an army, possessed by devils like himself, that traveled throughout all the regions and the coasts near and far, skinning humans. To invoke fear upon anyone who dared protest his leadership, his army strung up the skinless faces, arms and hands, and legs and feet on poles in all the villages for all to see, but they ate the raw human torsos in front of their victims' families. To maintain supremacy over the three main tribes, he established a council of tribal leaders called Los Antiguos to enforce his policies. At that moment, one of the FBI agents decided to ask one of the inevitable questions we all wanted an answer to. He asked Dr. Vinson how this man and his army died. Dr. Vinson's answer astounded all of us because he said there was no record of his death. The legend that had been passed from generation to generation alleged that this man and his army was so wicked they were allowed to pass through the portal of hell without experiencing human death. Supposedly, he and the other seventeen generals of his army are now Lords of the Underworld waiting to be summoned to wreak havoc on humanity at the behest of those who worshipped and sought them.

Several minutes of thought-provoked undisturbed silence passed before anyone decided to break it and ask the million dollar question all of us wanted to ask: why would anybody want to call these spirits up from hell? After a deep sigh and long pause, Dr. Vinson started speaking and directed our attentions to Revelation 12 and Genesis.

Revelation 12 details a war in heaven between Satan and God. Satan was overcome with jealously and decided to fight against God's eminence. Somehow, he managed to convince one-third of all the angels to side with him, but they were defeated and were cast out into the earth. Genesis deals with the fall of man in the Garden of Eden. Satan appeared to Eve in the form of a snake and persuaded her to eat from a tree God had forbidden her to eat from. Although he didn't speak directly to Adam, Adam ate from that same tree and sin entered the world, but God prophetically told Eve her seed would always be at odds with the seed of Satan. The only seed, or offspring, that exists, according to the Bible, without a man's reproductive contribution is Jesus. After we read these scriptures in unison, Dr. Vinson said he was truly a scientist and he believed that science had its place in the earth along with other inventions God had allowed man to make. However, he was a Christian and believed the Bible was the uncompromising word of God, and there were some things that science just could not diagnose or explain. I agreed fully with Dr. Vinson because I was a Christian and was fully persuaded Jesus Christ was Lord of all, whether they acknowledged him or not. However, the other officers and particularly the FBI agents didn't like what Dr. Vinson said, so they challenged him and pressed him to explain further what the Bible had to do with those dead politicians.

He obliged them and told them that all legends weren't completely fictional. There were relative truths to these legends, although there wasn't tangible evidence to prove them. He acknowledged there were evil spirits reserved in hell to terrorize the earth when God decided to release them, but there were also evil spirits presently in the earth controlling certain atmospheres bringing us closer to the end of "La Raza," the Race. For "La Raza" wasn't a race to take back the United States; instead it was a race to destroy humanity. If this gang, Los Serpientes, was worshipping and calling up these spirits along with all the other sin that existed, we were about to face the greatest and most diabolical event in all of modern human history, and no amount of human crafted weapons could stop it because spirits could not be fought with bullets.

The officers took a humanist approach and completely discounted everything Dr. Vinson said that was related to the Bible, but he was not disturbed nor did he seem surprised by their objections. It was almost as if he anticipated them. Consequently, I decided to refrain from offering my opinion at that point because it was obvious we were going have an unnecessary argument about the existence or nonexistence of God. While he was being bombarded with doubt, Dr. Vinson sat down and crossed his legs at the head of the conference table, unconcerned about the fact that most of the council members and the FBI agents were questioning his scruples. He carefully considered his answer before he spoke, but what he had to say in response to his critics was quite simple. He made it perfectly clear that faith was not tangible and everything tangible didn't require faith. It was simply a matter of what we chose to believe. However, we would be fools not to consider God's divine ability because there were too many things in existence that humans could not create and did not invent. Despite his opponents, I personally liked the man, and we began to form a close professional relationship after that meeting.

CHAPTER FOUR

A week after the meeting with Dr. Vinson, the Warden, a decorated Marine Corp veteran named Donovan Cuba, and several of the committee members, not including myself, decided to bring in some so-called theologians to add clarity to Dr. Vinson's biblical interpretations. I was personally against it because I didn't need some academic Christians with no personal relationship with Christ to explain the degrees of God's sovereignty to me, but I was overruled and outvoted on the matter. These folks showed up with clerical collars, large-print Bibles, briefcases, and a host of books they intended to use to argue their case, which insulted me because they were using the Bible to supplement what historians and scholars wrote as if they had to prove the Bible was true. Quite naturally, I counter-argued them because what they were doing was essentially blasphemy. How do you teach the Bible when you don't believe in it? How can you spend years studying about God and Christ and still not believe that they are real? How can you not have conviction? They had no conscience or shame about the fact that they were openly discrediting the very Bible they taught in colleges and prisons, for many of them were chaplains.

Dr. Vinson sat across the room the entire time, scribbling on the edges of paper in his notebook, clipping his fingernails, and humming to himself like a child who had no interest in being entertained by a company of unwanted visitors. I was furious! I felt like I was personally being attacked by a group of satanic lunatics who knew just enough to have an informed opinion but nothing of substance. I felt blood, from every part of my body, rushing to my head and throbbing in my temples. As a considerate consolation to me, Dr. Vinson grabbed my hand and suggested we leave to have tea in the break room while they argued and spewed ridiculous contradictions back and forth. We decided to go to the break room on the first floor because it was furthest away from the idiots in the conference room and because we knew we would have some moments of absolute privacy. I plopped down on the sofa and folded my arms while Dr. Vinson placed two tea bags in two mugs of hot water. Quietly, he walked over to the couch and gingerly sat down next to me and offered me a mug of tea. After a few minutes of eye rolling and head shaking silence, we looked at each and burst out laughing. It was hard to accept, but we knew we were dealing with some people who would never be convinced until they saw Jesus for themselves in all of his splendor and glory when it would be too late, so we agreed to start praying together in the mornings before the chaplains arrived. We also decided to keep many things to ourselves because our counterparts didn't share our convictions, so there was no point in arguing with them anymore.

Dr. Vinson began to tell me about many things he discovered that correlated with things he read in the Bible. In particular, he told me about an expedition he led several years ago in South America. He said, rather emphatically, that Christians, theologians, historians, and people in general have made the mistake of assuming Christianity arrived in the Americas when the Europeans came, but we were wrong. He took me to Joel 2:28 and started paraphrasing the passages as he explained his discovery. He said God consistently made it a point throughout the Bible, particularly the Old Testament, to send a messenger or at least a visual warning to nations before he destroyed them, but we have erroneously interpreted that passage of scripture because we associate God's decision to pour out his spirit upon all people before our era of humanity falls and Christ returns. On the contrary, God is quite fair. Therefore, he gives everybody an opportunity to repent before they are doomed to hell. Otherwise, they can't be saved in their lifetimes and that would contradict God's statements about saving anybody who called upon him in Romans 10. If people aren't given the chance to know God, how can they be saved by God? His point was that Jesus had to be presented in some way to ancient civilizations that existed in eras of mankind in the Americas before the Europeans arrived, so they would have an equal opportunity to accept him. I thought seriously about what he said and it made a lot of sense to me, although it was the first time I heard it expressed in that fashion, but his tangible, visible evidence bamboozled me; I couldn't speak for several minutes thereafter.

Dr. Vinson pulled out a photograph of his findings he had been carrying around in his wallet since the day he led that expedition. Before he showed it to me, he said the civilization they were unearthing during the expedition existed around 700 to 800 A.D.; he reminded me that historically, the Europeans didn't show up in the Americas until the fifteenth century. I nodded in full agreement with his statements. Suddenly, he held up the picture and asked me to think about how it was possible for a civilization to have a nativity scene in 700 to 800 A.D. if Christianity was not introduced to them until the Europeans arrived 700 to 800 years later. I nearly passed out when I saw the replica of baby Jesus, his mother Mary, and Joseph the natives carved out of stone.

My eyes were as big as silver dollars and my mouth wide open, trying to find something sensible to say, when I saw the picture. After a few moments, I actually felt guilty because I realized I was still very ignorant about many things that pertained to God. As Christians, we have a tendency to say we believe in things that relate to the awesomeness of God's power, but when we are faced with issues that are beyond human ability and have no scientific explanation, we discredit the proof and attribute it to some unnatural phenomena that has to do with aliens, prehistoric atomic collisions, or some other metaphysical crap rather than give God credit. Since that is the case, do we really believe in God or not? If we say that we do, why is it so hard for us to believe he has the ability to do things that exceed human knowledge? Why do we waste years trying to put God in a box that is limited to human ability and understanding? Dr. Vinson said we do this because we are creatures who exist in a world of tangibility; things that aren't tangible can at least be smelled, felt, or mentally perceived. Because we can't function outside of those parameters, we have a human need to make everything seem attainable. If we can't attain it, it must not be real.

I thought about this for several minutes while Dr. Vinson continued to explain what happened during the expedition. Naturally, he said he contacted other anthropologists to come and view the site, but when they arrived, they all dismissed the possibilities the natives carved the stone replica of the nativity scene but rather that alien intelligence came and duplicated the scene in an effort to show humans they weren't alone but were being watched by higher life forms. After the expedition was over, he was called upon to give a statement about the site to some committee of potentates who sat on the boards of various research-funding organizations and notable institutes. Based upon his research, the stone carvings were made by the natives. However, the other anthropologists pressed the idea that aliens carved the effigies, so the board members handsomely awarded Dr. Vinson for his discovery, but told him not to publicize anything about it that was tied to God, Christianity, or even religion period. They felt more comfortable telling the world that aliens had been carving statues as opposed to saying God had given prehistoric people a way out of sin. Dr. Vinson said that after that expedition, he decided not to seek funding from other organizations for his work anymore. He just started paying for it himself.

We continued sipping tea and talking for a while, mostly about his grandson, as we relaxed on the couch, gazing into empty spaces in the room and on the floor when we heard shouting in the hallway. As best we could tell, the chaplains and religious scholars who had been in the conference room upstairs separated to take a breather after a vicious argument about how much of the Bible was real and how much was simply symbolic. Dr. Vinson quickly slipped the picture from his expedition back into his wallet as the voices drew nearer to the break room. Realizing we were about to be seized and thwarted into a conversational diaspora, without speaking we kind of mutually agreed to act like we weren't aware they were approaching the break room. We casually started flipping through outdated magazines on the table, and Dr. Vinson grabbed the TV remote and turned on the news. While the weatherman was blabbing something about the possibility of rain, the unsolicited talking heads flung the door of the break room back and angrily stormed in. We both turned around on the couch and looked at them in a puzzled way like we were trying to figure why they were angry, but we heard enough of what they had to say in the hallway already.

One of them, Chaplain Beasley, an ample man with substantially large hands who loved touching people, was angry because he believed the scriptures Dr. Vinson used from Genesis and Revelation were merely metaphors that detailed the war between good and evil within man's inner-self. They were just stories to help people make the right choices in life, but one of the seminary theologians, Dr. Baker, told Chaplain Beasley he was stupid for believing that and he needed to have himself checked if he was seriously buying into that kind of crap. Dr. Vinson and I just sat there on the couch listening at all the ranting and raving from Chaplain Beasley, who was trying his best to find remarks low enough to discredit Dr. Baker with. His entourage of flunkies came with him to provide emotional, moral, or some other kind of support, but it didn't help. Dr. Vinson and I looked at each other, tuned them out, and turned back around to preoccupy ourselves with the room itself and whatever was in it. As far as we were concerned, they were all wrong, but there was no point in arguing to what degree they were wrong. We chose not to be involved any more than we absolutely had to be.

After they settled down, Chaplain Beasley came over and sat down in an armchair adjacent to the couch Dr. Vinson and I sat on and started telling Dr. Vinson how he was pleased to meet him and how he was familiar with his work, but he was wrong for taking the Bible literally and that he needed to spend more time doing biblical research if he was going to make definitive statements like that. Dr. Vinson, unmoved by Chaplain Beasley's statements, looked over the top of his wire-rim glasses and gave him a little smirk, but he remained silent with his legs crossed and arms folded on the couch. Chaplain Beasley continued with all of his loquacious, pejorative comments and hypocritical flattery, but Dr. Vinson ignored him and started asking me what the weatherman was saying while the chaplain was still talking. I did everything I could to keep from laughing, but it was so funny because the chaplain was so serious and he really did think Dr. Vinson cared about his opinions, and it hadn't occurred to him that Dr. Vinson had already mentally removed himself from his presence, so he just kept on talking.

Dr. Vinson started talking to me about other stuff, but the chaplain wouldn't shut up, so we got up and walked over to the sink and left the chaplain in the armchair next to the couch by himself. I was trying to keep a straight face, but by the time we got to the sink, I just burst out with uncontrollable laughter. The chaplain jumped up, trying to gather himself and recover from the embarrassment, and he and his flunkies headed toward the door once they realized they had run into a conversational brick wall, but before they could open the door, one of the FBI agents came in and said we all needed to come back to the conference room because the snitch, Dios, had some information that connected Los Serpientes to the killings that he wanted to share with us.

We were actually glad to see the agent because the chaplain was being overly chatty about nothing, and we were trying to minimize our rudeness by staying in the break room as opposed to walking out altogether. Needless to say, it also gave us a chance to interject dialogue about something else other than God since we disagreed on the subject. We went back to the conference room with the other committee members and waited for one of the guards to bring Dios into the room. The chaplain, still infuriated by Dr. Vinson's behavior, blurted out that perhaps Dr. Vinson and I shouldn't be there since we had differences with their opinions, but the Warden told him he was being vindictive and that we needed to stay because this particular meeting warranted our presence. We looked down at the table, grinning and digging in our fingers, trying to avoid making eye contact so we could maintain some kind of austerity, especially since the chaplain was frowning and turning beet red in the face. Just then, the guard brought Dios into the room along with some drawings and other stuff he had been working on.

The inmate was seated across the room from the committee members in a somewhat formal manner, but he didn't seem to mind. He started talking about an underground organization made up of free Hispanic citizens who were planning to orchestrate a riot within the next few weeks. He dissected the symbols on the drawings by the Scribe and told us where he believed the meeting would be held. According to Dios, these freelance rioters had met before, but this meeting was going to be different because they were planning to kidnap someone of importance to the United States and ransom them in exchange for territorial treaties the United States set up in the nineteenth century after their victory at the Alamo. Ironically, Dios said that in addition to bringing heavy artillery to this meeting, Hispanic leaders of this group invited some of the most distinguished witchcraft workers known in the Spanish world, and they intended to use them to conjure as much evil as possible against America. Chaplain Beasley asked Dios why having witches should be a concern of grave importance to America. The inmate looked puzzled and paused slightly open-mouthed with his head tilted to the side. He told the chaplain he didn't understand his question, so the chaplain repeated it. The inmate laughed at him, shaking his head and finger like an angry mother trying to contain herself in a department store when her child publicly embarrasses her. Dios told the chaplain that he was either stupid or blind because anyone, regardless of their religious beliefs, could clearly see America was not the "God-fearing" country it claimed to be and because it was spiritually weak; it was open for supernatural attack. Chaplain Beasley was absolutely livid at Dios's suggestion.

"How dare a prison inmate say that America is open to supernatural attack with all the churches, prominent TV evangelists, Christian organizations, and jail-house preachers in this country?"

Immediately, Dr. Vinson rendered Chaplain Beasley applause for his one-man show of bouts of hysterics. The FBI agents sighed and started tapping their pencils and pens on the table because they knew we were about to have round two of another intense discussion about God.

Dr. Vinson cleared his throat several times until everyone was silent. He slowly rose from his seat and stood behind the only empty chair at the table, looking over his glasses at everyone. Then he simply asked them why Dios's words sounded so foreign to them. Why were they so astonished and overwhelmed with disbelief? Actually, I wanted to know the same thing because it was obvious to me that there was a disconnection between America and God. Otherwise, we wouldn't have dead bodies, charred buildings, and mutilated politicians in the streets, but they didn't ask me what I thought, so I kept quiet, mostly to hear what they had to say, especially the chaplains and theologians.

Now the theologians chimed in and started talking about their knowledge of all the historical encounters with phantasms, and who said what, and who did what, and why it could or could not be true, and so on. The chaplains talked about the early church and monks and something somebody wrote that nobody knows anything about. I just sat there with my hands folded listening to them go back and forth with intellectual speculations about everything except what Dios said, so Dr. Vinson butted into their meaningless debate over religious trifles and asked them what they intended to do and how they intended to fight against these spirits that were being called up against America.

The FBI quickly interjected with how much could be budgeted by the government for troops and munitions. The theologians were yapping some historical nonsense about pieces of the Shroud of Turin, crosses, and holy water. The chaplains were talking about bringing in some big-named TV evangelist to broadcast a message on the airwaves. I looked at Dr. Vinson and told him he was so wrong for instigating this because we both knew this was going to happen. He gave me a devilish smile as he peered over the top of his glasses and took his seat. He leaned over and whispered to me he was enjoying playing the devil's advocate because as long as they were at odds with each other they would leave him alone. I knew he was right, but we were troubled because something terrible was about to happen, and the most prominent religious leaders in the country were so busy fighting over the past that they couldn't see the future.

Meanwhile, Dios sat there drawing on his arm with one of the markers he brought in with the stack of papers. Since most of the people in the room were yelling, he raised his hand to get their attention. When they finally acknowledged him, he asked to leave and go back to his cell. The Warden told him he couldn't leave yet because he wanted to know who the master mind was behind all the meetings and how this information was entering his prison. Dios told him that he didn't personally know any of the people in the outside world who were involved, but he did have a contact that brought pamphlets and other stuff to the prison. He said the guy worked for one of the delivery services that brought commercial cleaning products to the prison. He didn't know the man's name, but he would give him papers to give to the Snake's viceroys, which would undoubtedly get back to Cobra. If the Warden wanted to know the intricate details of what was happening, they needed to interrogate the delivery guy. Dios said that was all he knew. Before the Warden let him leave, he threatened him. He told Dios that if he breathed a word about the meeting to anybody, he would have him placed back in the general population and plant a mole to spread rumors that he was giving authorities information about Los Serpientes. We all knew that if that happened Dios would be dead within seventy-two hours after the rumors surfaced. It was no secret that Los Serpientes had influence, even with some of the guards in the prison. After Dios gave the Warden a basic description of the delivery guy, he was fed and taken back to his cell with his own private TV, DVD player, and a box full of movies, including soft porn. We had to find a way to keep him occupied in his cell because it was too dangerous and risky having him out on the yard. When we did let him go out, it was usually at night when all the other inmates were already in their cells and the guards on duty were members of the committee that we trusted.

Our first order of business now was to find out who the delivery guy was and whom he really worked for. The FBI made some calls to their headquarters and told whomever what they needed to hear to get the ball rolling. It was unanimously decided the FBI was the most qualified to handle an undercover operation like this, so all the committee members synchronized their radios and other communication devices to the same signal that only we knew. Next, we decided to plant a few undercover operatives in the general prison population to get close to the viceroys and other members of the Snake's gang so we could gather detailed information. The Warden also decided to secretly install some new surveillance cameras on the loading dock where all the shipments came in so we could see who this guy was and whom he dealt with inside. After we reached our initial agreement on how things were going to be handled, the Warden sent the theologians and the chaplains away until further notice and scheduled a private meeting with the committee members.

The warden initiated the dialogue by saying he was not a particularly religious man because he believed prison life had made him too callous to believe in anything he couldn't see. Moreover, he was really sorry he brought those so-called religious experts in because they only made things worse and we still didn't have a resolution. To my surprise, he also apologized to Dr. Vinson and added that after listening to all the hoopla and nonsense from the others, what Dr. Vinson said was about the only thing that really made sense. Since this was a religious issue, the Warden told Dr. Vinson he had all the liberty he needed to recommend someone from the religious world who was academically sound like himself to help us. Dr. Vinson humbly accepted the Warden's apology and told him he already had a few people in mind for the job, but he wouldn't tell us who they were until he made his final decision. Be that as it may, we finally reached an agreement we could all live with for the time being, but we had to act fast because we didn't know how much time we had or how strong this activist group really was. We were still a little stunned by the fact that the new terrorist group in America was now Hispanic.

Dr. Vinson and I decided to privately walk out along the prison grounds behind the administrative building where the employee sitting area was. It was quiet and filled with trees, flowers, and a man-made pond: the perfect spot for meditating. We sat down on one of the benches and stared at the grass until he broke the silence by asking me when I last spoke to my father and why I wasn't married. My name is Dr. Boudreaux, but he asked me if he could call me by my first name, which is Savanna. I told him I hadn't really spoken to my father in the last few days because I had been so caught up in all the excitement around the prison, and I wasn't married because I preferred being single at the time. He grabbed my hand and looked me in the face and said I really needed to talk to my father. When I asked him why, he simply said I would find out when I picked up the phone or whenever I decided to go see him. I thought it was strange that Dr. Vinson suggested that, but then again, our relationship was similar to that of a father-daughter relationship, so I knew he meant no harm. I decided to follow up on his suggestion, but instead of calling my father, I took off work for a few days so I could actually spend some time with both of my parents. Besides, the tranquil drive through the scenic countryside would do me some good anyway.

When I arrived at the house, my father was outside picking greens, carrots, and other vegetables he planted in the garden on the side of my house, for they had been staying at my house since the riots broke out few months ago. My mother was inside the house, cooking and playing the piano and humming between stirs in the pot of stew she had on the stove. They had been retired for a few years, but they were still quite active. My parents were kind-hearted, reserved people with traditional Pentecostal values, but they were non-judgmental and they didn't excite easily behind bad news. Not to mention, they had lived too long to be overwhelmed by anything new. Although they were getting older, their minds were extremely sharp, and they could still recall things that happened when I was a child that even I didn't remember, which made talking to them soothing. Needless to say, they were glad to see me but, as usual, they gave me several reasons why they preferred I teach in a tradition school environment. However, we never argued about where I worked as long as they believed I was happy.

After I took my bags to my bedroom, I helped my mother peel and dice potatoes for the stew while my father diced the onions and carrots and updated me on all the births, deaths, and weddings in the family. He kept up with these kinds of things since he was better at remembering names. When my father temporarily left the room to get all the funeral programs and obituaries he collected since the last time we saw each other, my mother started with her standard comments about why she believed I needed to settle down and get married soon, how I would never meet the right man if I continued to spend all my time around criminals, and if I did meet Mr. Right anytime soon, I might not be mentally fit for him after spending so much time around the criminally insane. I could always count on my mother to remind me that my biological clock was ticking; I was still single, and close to forty. My father, on the other hand, didn't seem to mind because he'd rather see me single and satisfied than married and miserable. Besides, he accepted years ago that I was a free-spirited person who refused to be tied down to something or someone I didn't care for, so he never pressed the issue. I knew my mother meant well, too, but she just didn't understand that marriage wasn't the measure of all things for me. It was an option, not an obligation.

Eventually, we got around to setting the table and eating some homemade beef stew with cornbread and a glass of freshly squeezed lemonade. My father talked about all the things going on in the world that he had heard about or seen on the news and all the books he read. My parents still pastored a church and at one time, my father was the dean of a Christian college. He was still an avid reader and could expound on just about anything at any given time. My mother read a lot as well, but she mostly busied herself with her music and other projects around the house that fit her personality and the values of her upbringing. Even so, we talked about a little bit of everything, including recent events at the prison. As one might expect, nothing I said was a jaw-dropper for them. In fact, they weren't the least bit surprised by any of it. They reminded me that Jesus's second coming was soon and that things were going to get worse before he came. I knew they were right, and having them as parents made me glad all the more that I was a preacher's kid because I felt like they gave me a head start in life. I didn't know everything about the future of the world, but I knew enough about God to make good choices about my own future.

Over the course of our conversation, I told my father about Chaplain Beasley and all the theologians the Warden brought in. My father told me to pray for them because they were deceived, just like all the other people in the world who didn't believe Christ was the savior of this world. He told me he met many Christianity professors during his tenure at the college who studied the Bible religiously because of their profession, but they never established a personal relationship with God. He said it used to grieve him to see them because their hearts were never pricked by the truth even though they read it every day. At that point, it seemed like he was getting a little emotional, but he brought himself back to a level place long enough to prop his feet up in his recliner and eat a piece of my mother's chocolate cake.

After I finished the dishes and folded up the laundry my mother laid across the couch, I decided to approach my father a little more intently with information about the murders. He always seemed to have the right words at any given time, even when he didn't know all the particulars about what happened. I showed him just a couple of the pictures of the crime scenes with the missing torsos; immediately, he told me that he had a dream about something similar, which led him to do some private research about the matter. He also said that he decided to pray, fast, and search the Bible for answers. Later, he also said he had contacted scientists and other professionals who had published or documented information on the same subject in an effort to find as many clues as he possibly could to help him unravel the hidden mysteries in his dream.

After seven days of fasting, my father said God told him that America was going to war, but this time the war would be on American soil. For some reason, I wasn't shocked to hear this news. It was as if I was expecting him to say this, and I knew he was dead serious about what he said. My father wasn't the type of Christian who put God's name in front of everything he read or heard, but when he did hear from God, you could take his words to the bank and cash them every single time. Intrigued by this, I decided to search and pray for specific information as well so I could better understand what was about to happen.

Before I went to bed, I decided to call Dr. Vinson to check on him and let him know I made it home safely. As usual, our conversation was pleasant but brief. However, before he released the line, he asked me if my father had told me about his dream. When I asked him how he knew my father, he said they had spoken on the phone a few times after my father sent him an email request a few months ago for some information about ritual killings that he published from one of his expeditions, so his suggestion to me in the sitting area was not coincidental. He admitted they hadn't formally met, but they kept in touch with each other from time to time since they were both fond of certain Christian writers. Consequently, I called my father into the room and told him I knew Dr. Vinson and handed him the phone. It was a wonderful surprise to know they were familiar with each other, but it really shouldn't have been a surprise at all because they acted very similar. I should've guessed though that Dr. Vinson knew a little more than he let on, but everything was good, so I wasn't worried about it.

After they finished speaking, I told my father all about him and how he carried on in the meetings with the experts. My father was overcome with laughter, but he was also glad somebody stood up for what was right. We talked a little bit more about the murders and some of the research information he got from Dr. Vinson, and then we prayed together. Finally, we made some preliminary plans to do some things the next day, exchanged hugs and "I love yous," and called it a night.

CHAPTER FIVE

Several weeks had passed since the riots had stopped, and the remaining members of the government finally convened in Washington to present a solution to the country's immigration problem. The crooked deportation laws set up by southern politicians were denounced, and the Senate and Congress finally reached a mutual agreement about what to do. They decided the least expensive way to keep all the immigrants and their families together in this country was to resettle them. There was enough uninhabited land in the southern states that could be developed and used for resettlement to accommodate the undocumented residents. The government initially decided to set up a system to identify all the undocumented alien residents, so that those who were already living in America before the resettlement idea was initiated were given a red ID card. They would be allowed to bring only members of their immediate families into the country to live in the new settlement areas. Those family members would be given a blue ID card, except for those who were under the age of eighteen. They were given a white ID card. This idea was formerly presented by the President, unanimously agreed upon by the Senate and Congress, and was overwhelmingly supported by United States citizens with a majority vote of 90 percent.

After the Resettlement Bill was passed, all the border states sent out inspectors to survey the uninhabited parts of their states to ensure the country wasn't repeating the same mistake with this group as it had done before when Native Americans were resettled. When the survey crews finished surveying the land, the governors drew up new legal agreements, approved by their state legislators, on how the settlement areas would be zoned, governed, taxed, and politically represented. Before estimates of the work expenses were put forth, contractors were already lining up like flies on a dumpster behind a restaurant to bid for government labor contracts. Some of them saw this as an opportunity to get rich. However, the government had previously expressed concerns about public bidding for labor contracts because the country was still financially strapped. We really couldn't afford to pay long-term labor contracts, so members of Congress and the Senate reached a majority decision to use the inmate work force for the bulk of the work and contract only a small amount of it to individual contractors. Once again, the preponderance of American citizens thought the decision was fair and agreed that inmates should be doing most of the work, since our tax dollars housed, fed, clothed, and educated them. Of course, there was a waiting process in all of this because the government had to decide which states would be first on the resettlement list and which prisons within those states would be chosen for the work. Logically, the word about the resettlement project spread throughout the prisons, and the inmates, particularly Los Serpientes, stopped rioting for a while because they thought the resettlement idea was a step in the right direction. Resettling immigrants certainly didn't help us gather leads to resolve the mutilation issue with the dead politicians from the riots, but for the time being the issue was temporarily vacated.

After a few weeks of deliberation, the government decided to begin the work from the west coast to the east coast because the border-states further west were larger states with larger Hispanic populations and larger prison populations. Consequently, California, Arizona, and Texas were chosen first for resettlement construction. The decision was settled, and my prison was one of the first to be selected in the resettlement project. We had a large population of inmates, and more than half of them were skilled in some form of carpentry, public works, or electrical trades. I was actually glad we were chosen. I felt it would be good for the inmates to finally see something different and to have an opportunity to put their skills to use. Besides, some of these inmates hadn't seen the outside world in over twenty years. Sadly, not all of the prison staff members were glad about it.

Some of them were really skeptical about having inmate work crews outside the prison walls because they would have access to open land space and might escape. I wasn't concerned about them escaping because the only place they could go would be to Mexico, but they would have to survive night predators like snakes, wolves, and coyotes, along with the desert heat without food or water for days, just to get there. Unless they knew exactly where they were going and had food provisions stored up somewhere close by, they weren't going to survive. But even if we were increasing the risk of inmate escape, I believed the government's intentions were good this time and I was willing to support them. Besides, working to build something positive was a lot better than just having inmates sit around for twenty years or so in cages doing nothing.

Later, our state governor, Trevor Schwartz, sent some envoys throughout the state to all the prisons that had been selected to participate in Project IRZ: Immigrant Resettlement Zone. That was the official name it was given after it had gone through all levels of government and legally approved. The envoys had a general meeting with the prison population at large to make the announcement but afterward had private meetings with staff members and the Special Crimes Committee. In the committee meeting we had, the envoys made us fully aware they were not the average garden variety emissaries sent to congratulate us for being selected. These guys were from some sect of law enforcement or the military who were knowledgeable in explosives, weapons, combat tactics, and interrogation. They talked to us at length and showed us films of possible weapons and drugs commonly transported through the area we were assigned to, prostitution rings, cartel mules, counterfeit currency, and possible connections to Los Serpientes. In short, this Immigrant Resettlement Zone project wasn't just about pacifying Hispanic alien residents; it was also a trap to catch Los Serpientes and their connections. As a result, we were to be armed at all times and to operate on the highest level of alert until given further notice. We were given maps of our work and camp locations with specific detailed instructions about what to do if we saw any illegal aliens crossing the border into the United States near our sites or if an inmate made an attempt to escape. Our instructions were simple but clear: shoot them.

After the briefings with the envoys, we started making mass preparations for transport to our camp and work sites, which included daily lengthy meetings with federal, state, and county officials. Nearly two months had passed before our prison was finally given a transport date so we could begin working. Before the main body was mobilized, a reconnaissance team was sent first to investigate the area for possible safety hazards and escape routes and also to set up portable storage lockers for all the equipment we were taking and given by the Department of Transportation and privately owned construction companies. Once they scouted the area, an advance work party went in and set up all the tents, portable showers, mobile kitchen trailers, outdoor dining equipment, mobile commissaries, mobile laundry facilities, outdoor medical facilities, and the central control units at the camp and work sites. Sergeant Thomas headed the advance party. The Warden wanted his best man on the ground to greet the inmates when they arrived.

After the camp was set up, the delivery trucks came and dropped off portable toilets, food, more tools and equipment, medicals supplies, and some leisure items for the inmates to entertain themselves with when they had down time on their days off. While all this was going on outside the prison, we were vaccinating and checking for allergies, updating medical records, issuing new ID cards, coordinating mail drops and family visitation for the sites, and everything else we could think of inside the prison. Work crews were working nearly sixteen hours a day cleaning that compound from top to bottom, and we had an additional security team contracted to work with us during this transitional period to ensure there were no more breaches of security than the preexisting ones.

These preparations were tedious but necessary because we were literally taking tens of thousands of convicts out of their assigned prisons to work on project sites in the middle of nowhere, far from civilization. The sites had to be perpetually secured by armed guards working shifts in eight to twelve hour rotations. Every tool down to the last nail had to be accounted for daily. The head count still had to be done three times a day on the site as it was done behind bars. Safety glasses, hard hats, steel-toed boots, and gloves had to be issued to and worn by everyone entering the work site without regard for whom they were. Staff members had to carry loaded weapons and radios at all times, even to take a shower or to use the bathroom. Protocol had to be followed to the letter, and there was no latitude given for mistakes. It goes without question that there was a lot of excitement and nervous tension in the air as we made ready to leave our unit. The government had a lot riding on these projects, and it was ultimately our duty to ensure this mission; it was critical to our unit, critical to future residents of this area, and critical to our country at large that this was carried out successfully.

The day of our departure had finally arrived, and I was scheduled to ride in a private vehicle with other members of the trail party. I inquired about Dr. Vinson but was told he would be joining us later for reasons unknown. We deliberately stayed behind after the main body left the prison to ensure that all the cells, loading dock, and supply areas were secured. There were only a handful of folk who stayed behind at the prison, mostly disabled and wounded inmates or inmates who were HIV positive and just enough staff members to care for them. The other 26,000 inmates and 4,000 staff members left earlier for the camp, but not all at once. The inmates had already been segregated a few days earlier according to their particular skills and trade, so there were four main groups evenly divided with 6,500 inmates and 1,000 staff members in each group. These groups were further subdivided into five smaller groups of 1,300 inmates with 200 staff members assigned to the subset. They were sectioned into five main work groups with colored overalls: carpentry wore brown, public works wore blue, utilities wore yellow, general maintenance wore green, and culinary wore white.

The camp was situated such that the control unit was in the center of the camp and the inmate tents circled the control unit; one group occupied the tents on the north side, another on the east side, another on the south side, and the last group on the west side. Since there were five subdivisions within the inmate sections, they were given ID numbers according to which section they lived in and the work group they were assigned to, so the inmate with the number N21300 was identified as the 1300th member assigned to work group two in the north section and so on. The staff members pitched their tents in a circle around the inmates, and the exterior guards had tents on the outskirts of the camp enclosing the staff members. Thus, the camp resembled a bull's eye.

The outdated buses with the caged tinted windows started arriving earlier that day, about 0400 in the morning, to haul the inmates and staff members to a site they would call home for the next two or three years. By 0800, all 500 of the buses were parked along the stretch of highway in front of the main gate, waiting to be signaled in for loading. However, before anybody, inmate or staff member, walked out of the prison, there was a massive prison-wide shakedown to ensure contraband did not enter our camp or work sites. Every inmate on our compound had to strip down to his nakedness and endure thorough cavity searchers. Most of the heterosexual inmates loathed the cavity searches because they were so intrusive and demeaning, but they were absolutely necessary for the well, sick, disabled, blind, deaf, heterosexual, and homosexual alike. I have personally witnessed discoveries of illegal drugs, weapons, cell phones, and other items considered contraband as the result of cavity searches during a shakedown. You'd be amazed at how long a person can conceal an object inside their body until he is forced to bend over and cough. When I first began working in the prison, I thought the cavity searches were one of the most grotesque forms of security searches that existed. Now, it's just another procedure we use for protection.

That being said, once the shakedown ordeal was finished, the first group of inmates who were going to be housed on the west side of the camp loaded the first 125 buses. The total trip time from our prison to the campsite was two hours, so the buses were staggered in two hour intervals. The Warden felt this was the best way to manage crowd control because it was a lot easier to account for 125 busloads of inmates than it was to account for 500 at one time. Since the inmates were wearing colored overalls, all they had to do was assemble with their workgroup and wait for further instructions after they arrived. To make the transition smoother and less time consuming, as soon as the buses arrived on site, the inmates were immediately filed over to the storage lockers to pick up their cots, blankets and pillows, safety equipment, and toiletries. By the time the second set of buses arrived, the first group of inmates had nearly finished picking up all their gear, so the line wasn't that long for the next group, and so on.

The last group left our prison unit about 5:00 PM and arrived on site just in time for dinner. After the trail party finished wrapping things up at the unit, we finally left, heading for the camp around 6:30 PM. We made a few stops along the way, so our trip ended up being closer to three hours, but it wasn't bad. I was glad when we were finally able to leave because it just seemed like the hardest part of our day was finally over. I was so exhausted, but it was more from anticipation and preparation than the actual move. Since we were leaving on a Friday, we had Saturday and Sunday to attend more boring but mandatory meetings, settle in, and rest. I just wanted to get my cot, shower, and lay down.

We pulled into the campsite about 9:00 PM. By that time, all the inmates and staff members had eaten dinner at their respective dining facilities and were heading for the showers. The Special Crimes

Committees had one more meeting we needed to attend that night before we could turn in. The meeting was about the FBI operatives we had planted in the general population a few months ago when the mutilated politicians were found during the riots. Since prison life had been relatively quiet the last few weeks and they had blended in so well, I had almost forgotten about them, but they too were numbered among the inmates and segregated into a work group. Some of them didn't know how to do the jobs they were chosen for, so we had to make some minor adjustments to keep the numbers balanced between the work groups. However, that was but a small thing. Our primary reason for meeting was to gain insight on what they had discovered about Los Serpientes since they had been planted in the prison.

Federal agents Joey Trevino, Russell Alvarez, Daniel La Paz, Ramón Ducati, Jason Van der Hogan, Neal Freeman, and Quinton Alexander had been working undercover in our prison for several months since the pictures of the mutilated politicians began circulating. Trevino and Ducati hung out with Los Serpientes; Alvarez was planted in the Ecumenical Community; Van der Hogan joined the Woods; Freeman was affiliated with the Black Knights; Alexander associated with the Islamic Brotherhood, and La Paz was just a member of the general population. As expected, none of the agents volunteered to infiltrate the She-males, so we had to rely on their associations with the other prison social groups to find out whether She-males were involved in any way with the murders.

The Warden purposely had the agents selected for some makeshift detail so we could separate them from the main body and talk to them and so they would have access to the control unit without casting suspicion upon themselves. Since we were working together with the FBI, every so many weeks, the agents had to file reports to their superiors documenting their findings about the murders. It was relatively easy to segregate them back at the prison because the complex is so large. Now that we were outside at a smaller campsite, we had to move them strategically so things still looked normal. Consequently, they were secretly brought into a private tent by Sergeant Thomas, the Warden's right-hand man, which was set up strictly for the Special Crimes Committee on the perimeter of the camp. The agents arrived with buckets, brooms, dusting rags, and cleaning stuff as if they were really going to be put to work. Once they were safely inside and a guard was posted outside the tent, they set their cleaning props down and pulled out some small notebooks they were using to keep tabs on what was happening in our prison. Agents Trevino and Ducati had been planted in Los Serpientes, so they were the first to tell us what they had found.

Trevino said that Los Serpientes was a highly organized criminal enterprise with generals, captains, lieutenants, and other lower-ranking individuals like the military. Every person within a specified rank structure had an individual job and that was their only job, but those jobs were determined by what zone of the country they were located in. For example, the generals in the west may be responsible for trafficking illegal drugs into the country. However, the generals in the east may be responsible for trafficking munitions. The generals in the north may be responsible for acquiring illegal documents like passports, birth certificates, and driver licenses. The generals in the south may be the clean-up crew who makes sure Los Serpientes' enemies are killed and witnesses disappear. No two generals from different regions have the same job. Likewise, generals from the same region have variations within their jobs, although the overall mission is the same. So if, hypothetically, the generals in the west are supposed to traffic illegal drugs, one general maybe in charge of cocaine, another in charge of heroine, another methamphetamines, another marijuana, and so on.

Aside from the organizational structure of the gang, they were also materially wealthy and very influential, especially with affluent people. According to Trevino and Ducati, Los Serpientes had access to planes, ships, and ground transportation in order to move their drugs and weapons. They had over-the-road trucking companies, bakeries, floral shops, jewelers, toy stores, and delivery services set up as fronts all over the United States, functioning in unison to form a massive network of crime that no one ever suspected. We hated to hear what the agents said because, essentially, it meant that America's internal security was weak. However, it really didn't come as a surprise because people have been smuggling drugs and other illegal items into the United States for years, but Los Serpientes are a bit more sophisticated than most of the operations that have been discovered in the last fifteen to twenty years.

The agents also said that Los Serpientes weren't working alone inside the prison. In fact, they have a lot of white-collar help from people outside the prison who are connected to some of the Woods inside, which explains why the Woods are the only prison social group with access to everything and they do not have to lower their prices to match another gang's offer. Ducati said that after the Woods introduced Los Serpientes' contacts to some of their "corporate sponsors" who facilitated Los Serpientes in bribery, forgery, and other illegal activities, Cobra, Los Serpientes' leader, issued a national order of protection for the Woods, which means they are off limits to everybody in the national prison system. The Warden was flabbergasted at the news, along with everybody else in that tent, because we all knew the only way a gang's national order of protection could be upheld was if they had dirty prison guards working with them. Now we had a major problem because we didn't know who the dirty guards were in our prison, and they could've been members of the Special Crimes Committee leaking information to Los Serpientes all along. However, since Van der Hogan had been planted in the Woods' group, we were all hoping he could shed some light on how the Woods were connected to this.

Van der Hogan, a thin but exceptionally handsome agent with dirty blond hair and green eyes, was given an apprentice position within the Woods' organization by none other than the Woods' leader, Nigel Carter. Nigel was an interesting but toxic character who was intellectually brilliant but psychologically lethal. Nigel Carter had a master's degree in psychology but was convicted of second degree murder. Mr. Carter actually should have been placed on the death row list because he plotted and conspired his wife's murder for almost a year before he finally stabbed her to death, severed her body into small pieces, and set fire to their home to disguise the murder, all because his wife would not take money from the estate she inherited from her family to finance some investment scheme Nigel was involved in that she wasn't comfortable with. In some way, Nigel Carter, representing himself in the courtroom, was able to convince the jury he killed his wife in a moment of temporary insanity. His charges were reduced to second-degree murder, and he was sentenced to twenty-five years in prison. Since he has served seven of those years already, he'll be up for parole in five more years. It's sad but true. Even so, Nigel is extremely dangerous, not that he would ever fight or kill anyone in prison himself, but he's dangerous because he's intelligent and conniving enough to prey on the weaknesses of other gullible humans and use them as his minions. Oddly, Van der Hogan said Nigel chose him as an apprentice because he had nice penmanship. Nigel, the psychologist, studied facial expressions and handwriting so he could manipulate people around him, but Van der Hogan was the perfect match. He had a master's degree in forensic psychology and was an expert at spotting pathological disorders.

Van der Hogan said the Woods had some kind of obscure arrangement with members of the Ecumenical Community. He didn't know all the details yet, but as far as he knew at the current moment, the Woods had some outside contacts in the religious world that posed as unsuspecting visiting clergy members coming to have Bible study in the prison with members of the Ecumenical Community. Since the clergymen are licensed and ordained elders in the church world, they are hardly ever searched for contraband. Let's face it, nobody would really guess that a pastor would be carrying several grams of cocaine or heroin in a hidden passage in his Bible. However, to everyone's surprise, that's exactly what some of the ministers were doing. The drugs actually belong to Los Serpientes, but the Woods and the Ecumenical Community are helping them bring the drugs into the prison for distribution for a small cut of the profits and protection.

Van der Hogan's findings helped us put a few of the puzzle pieces together, but we were still stumped because none of this could flow smoothly without the help of some dirty prison guards. We were also perplexed about Los Serpientes' movements because it didn't make sense for them to have their drugs brought to the prison for distribution when it was much easier to just distribute them from the streets. What was so important about bringing the drugs to prison?

The Warden, a former military tactician, was determined to snuff out the dirty prison guards and squash the entire gang drugs and murder operation in our prison. He asked the other agents, Freeman and Alexander, if they had any news from the Black Knights and the Islamic Brotherhood that would help us. Both of the agents stated their information was merely circumstantial nonsense. None of it could be considered a solid lead yet. However, there was a rumor surfacing that something big was going to happen back at the prison soon. The overall plan hadn't been mapped out yet, but the gangs definitely had something in the works. The Warden commissioned Freeman and Alexander to get as close as possible to the leaders of the Black Knights and the Islamic Brotherhood so they could at least get a timeframe on what was expected to happen. In addition, the Warden wanted them to find out who the gangs' treasurers were because the Black Knights and the Islamic Brotherhood were notorious for bribing guards. If the agents could find out who held the money, they could follow the money trail and find the guards who were being paid. Last, but certainly not least, La Paz interjected with probably the most critical piece of information that could help us infiltrate Los Serpientes.

La Paz had been planted within the general population without any specific gang affiliations. He presented himself as the typical low-key, quiet inmate who is just trying to serve his time with as little friction as possible. He deliberately does things habitually so he can be labeled non-threatening and predictable, which allows him to easily gain other inmates' trust. But La Paz possesses a particular skill that Los Serpientes needs to keep their communication chain strong: he can draw. Everybody knows Los Serpientes uses an artist they call a scribe to embed messages in tattoo drawings. This is their main form of communication, and it's quite effective because the only way we can really decipher their messages is if one of the gang members is banished and comes to us for protection in exchange for information. The only other way we have been able to get small bits and pieces of information is by listening to Los Serpientes' phone calls and reading letters they send to and receive from the outside.

Every three or four years, Los Serpientes adds a new scribe to their payroll so they can diversify their tattoo styles. They don't want anybody to get used to seeing a certain tattoo style too long because they figure the hidden messages might eventually be decoded if they don't change the style. When Los Serpientes are ready to start recruiting new artists, they send gang members to canvas the arts and crafts classes in the prison. They may even have a sudden death drawing competition, depending on how many inmates they have vying for the position. Most inmates who can draw consider it an honor to be a scribe because the position carries a lot of weight, but it's also treacherous because the scribe, like the runner, knows too much, and once the scribe losses his usefulness, he becomes a target of opposition.

That being the case, La Paz said one the gang members took some of his drawings to Cobra to see if he could get approved for a scribe position within the gang. Until he was officially selected, he was ordered to shadow one of the current scribes so he could be taught the language behind the tattoos. Since he had just begun shadowing the scribe, he didn't know enough to put phrases together yet. He was learning the symbols the way a small child would learn the alphabet: one letter at a time. However, he wrote everything down and even duplicated the symbols in his notebook so he could later teach us what he was learning. The Warden, eager to get a head start on the decoding process although we had a steep learning curve, pulled out some old pictures of tattoo drawings he kept from a previous committee meeting to see if we could translate some information with the few symbols La Paz could read. As one might guess, it was a slow and laborious process. Nevertheless, we were able to determine that some outside contact for Los Serpientes was supposed to be bringing a major shipment of something to our prison. Recalling a previous conversation we had with Dios, Los Serpientes' old runner, the Warden alluded to the delivery guy being the most likely outside contact for this job. With that, we mutually agreed to set a trap for the dirty guards, the delivery guy, the Woods, and the Ecumenical Community, and Los Serpientes would be used as the bait.

Since we had obvious security issues, the Warden came up with an idea to weed out the weak links among the committee members. There were twelve of us in all assigned to the committee, but only eleven of us were there, so he wrote down twelve different security passwords on twelve small slips of paper. He folded up the slips of paper and placed them in a hat. When the last slip of paper was placed in the hat, he asked us to step outside the tent and wait for him to call us back one by one alphabetically, so we all got up and walked outside. One by one, the Warden called out a name, and that person had to come into the tent alone and pull a slip of paper from the hat, and the Warden recorded that person's password down in a secret place. After the Warden documented the password, the slip of paper was destroyed, so the only person who knew everybody's password was the Warden. After each individual committee member was assigned a password, we stepped outside the tent again, one by one, and waited until all eleven of us had gone through this process. When it was finished, the Warden called us back inside and we began strategizing our next move like nothing had just happened.

CHAPTER SIX

It was early Sunday morning and it was the last day we had to rest and plan before our first official day of construction began. The Warden had already scheduled a meeting for the committee members that evening to go over some preliminary details about what we were planning to do going forward. I was particularly concerned about this meeting because the Warden planned to invite Cobra, the leader of Los Serpientes, to attend. The Warden decided to use a little reverse psychology to thank Cobra for keeping his gang under subjection while the government deliberated on the ins and outs of Project IRZ. He also wanted to put a bug in Cobra's ear that one or some of his disciples may not have been that faithful to him. He intended to make Cobra think some of his affiliates were snitching, so Los Serpientes' every move was going to be thoroughly scrutinized as long as we were at this campsite. He knew Cobra was not going to take the news lightly. He also knew Cobra would make immediate, drastic changes to seal any leaks in his organization by any means necessary. To stir up Cobra's sense of paranoia even further, the Warden decided to use some inmates to spread false information, knowing full well that the rumors would spread like wild fire. Thus, the trap would be laid, and it was just a matter of time before the big spider was caught in his own web of crime.

It was already eight o'clock, and I was a little out of sync with things because normally I would have already gone running, showered, and have eaten by this time. Since we were at the camp, I could only run during daylight hours on a two-mile segment of the road that had been completely sealed off for the campsite. It wasn't all that bad though because I was actually able to get an additional two hours of sleep before I got up. When I did finally get up, I ran my usual two-mile stretch and then headed for the shower. By the time I got dressed and went to the dining area, Dr. Vinson was already there sitting at a table alone, waiting for me with a couple of steaming hot mugs of dark roast coffee. It took a few minutes for me to get my ham and cheese omelet, hash browns, and wheat toast from the chow line, and, of course, I stopped by the beverage counter for some fresh juice on my way to the table. When I got a few feet from the table, Dr. Vinson, being the gentlemen he is who still believes in chivalry, stood and gently took my plate and set it down on the table for me. I was very happy to see him but was quite curious about why he didn't ride with the trail party Friday and delayed his arrival until Saturday evening. As a matter of fact, I was told he came in very late last night after everyone was asleep. But he didn't act as if anything was wrong, and, as usual, he talked about his grandson in his casual way, looking over the wire-rim glasses he had resting on the tip of his nose. By this time, I knew him well enough to assume he probably did have something important to tell me, but it wasn't the right time or place just yet, so I didn't press him for information.

We sat there eating and talking about our presumptions over this immigration project and the whole campsite business. We both agreed it was definitely going to be unpredictable, and we should not be shocked by anything that happened once the work commenced. Incidentally, I asked Dr. Vinson if he had gotten his password from the Warden and if he had been brought up to speed with all the new information the FBI agents had given us Friday evening. He affirmed that the Warden had briefed him on all the happenings, but he didn't personally believe all of what he was told, especially about Los Serpientes bringing drugs to the prison. This was a meticulous gang with influence in corporate America and even in some areas of Congress; they wouldn't be careless enough to risk getting caught with their own dope in a penitentiary facility. It just didn't make sense to him, and the more he kept talking about it, it made even less sense to me now than it did when I was first told. I'm not a law enforcement officer, but I know something didn't seem right about it. In fact, it sounded so ridiculous it is almost as if it's a lie deliberately planted to set up the committee members. I would even venture to say now that it is very possible that Los Serpientes knows or suspects that there are undercover officers working within the prison population. It wouldn't be a great surprise if they knew though, especially since we had dirty prison guards accepting bribes.

After about an hour or so, Dr. Vinson and I decided to bottle up our discontent and save it for the meeting later that evening. We left the dining area to take a casual stroll around the perimeter of the camp. We were definitely out in the country miles away from civilization, but the place was naturally beautiful and we both loved trees and rocky landscapes. When we reached the edge of the southern end of the camp, Dr. Vinson pulled out a camera so he could take pictures of the trees and blossoming plants that dotted the horizon. We didn't venture that far off, but we did walk around part of the area that was surveyed for construction. The slope stakes were sticking out of the ground with yellow, orange, and blue ribbons tied around them, and there were several trees with red ribbons tied around them as well that were going to be cleared tomorrow so the foundation of the resettlement zone could be laid.

We continued to walk through part of the area closest to the camp where the brush wasn't as thick. We found a little pond with some very small fish and tadpoles swimming near the surface. There were birds of various sorts chirping loudly from the treetops while an assortment of lizards zigzagged across the ground at the strange sound of human feet parading around through their home. As we casually trekked a little further out, we both noticed something very odd that didn't blend with the natural tapestry of this area. There was a clearing of some sort right in the middle of all those trees and shrub, and it just didn't seem like it belonged there. It wasn't very big, but it was quite noticeable because all the trees and vines and plants that were growing along the ground everywhere else did not exist there. Everything in this clearing was dead. It was just wide-open space with dirt and some rocks of various sizes on the ground in no discernible order. There was no life in this clearing at all. Dr. Vinson's anthropology expertise kicked in, and we started looking for signs of life to see if maybe we had stumbled upon a segment of a former village or something. Before we could thoroughly examine the area, the Warden started calling us on our two-way radios so we had to go back to the camp, but we vowed to come back to the clearing to investigate.

When Dr. Vinson and I arrived at the control unit in the center of the camp, Sergeant Thomas met up with us outside the tent and told us the Warden was about to call our meeting with Cobra now instead waiting until later. He said the Warden had to attend a last-minute meeting this afternoon that the governor had arranged so he could talk to all the prison wardens involved in this project. Dr. Vinson didn't seem too concerned, but I wasn't psychologically prepared to meet Cobra now. I had heard so many bad things about him and had seen the end results of his wrath against other people but never had any personal dealings with him. I had seen him several times on the compound at a distance, and he looks distorted in an unnatural way because he's covered with tattoos from his shaved head to the bottom of his feet. He looks like a walking comic strip or hieroglyphic wall.

It's eerie just looking at him from a distance. It makes you wonder what would drive a person to draw on themselves or mar their flesh to that degree. I could see having a few tattoos here and there, but he is literally covered with so many tattoos that he could walk around completely nude publicly and no one would really know the difference. I remember watching a taped interview one of the chaplains conducted with him several years ago after we found one of Los Serpientes' victims. He was making so many weird facial movements that his tattoos intensified his creepiness, making it difficult for the chaplain to continue the interview. To this day, we still don't know whether he has real eyebrows or not.

Since I've only seen him from afar, I can't really say that he's tall, but I can say that he's not a large man. He's just extremely unusual, but I suppose he uses his mystique to compensate for some other shortcomings or to embellish his reputation as a madman. Whatever the case may be, the committee members began gradually filing into the tent for the impromptu meeting with the Warden. All twelve of us arrived before the Warden finally showed up. He seemed pressed for time, but he was still able to get the gist of what he wanted to say out. At that point, I was informed that some of the inmates voiced concerns about the fact that they were enrolled in college courses prior to the project selection. They either received educational grants or had family members paying their tuition. Now that this project was official, they weren't going to be able to attend school unless we had provisional classes in some of the tents on the campsite. Since I was the senior professor, the Warden made it clear that this was my baby and I had full control over how it was to be handled. I asked the Warden to give me a week to make preparations since the information came on such short notice. I assured him that by the beginning of the second week of work, we would have an official class schedule ready so the inmates wouldn't forego any semesters of school.

Our next order of business had to do with the FBI agents working undercover in our prison. The Warden flat out told us he didn't trust some of them and felt like one or some of them were playing both sides against the middle. After he said that, all the eyebrows in that tent went up. The Warden wasn't particularly an opinionated person, but if he told you he believed something was either this way or that way, you could trust it was genuine. As to be expected, all the inquiring minds in that tent wanted to know what led the Warden to suspect we were being played by the agents. The Warden told us he didn't have enough concrete evidence to prove his hunch yet, but he decided to take an additional precaution and plant his own mole in the general population. But this time, nobody would know who the mole was except the Warden. Dr. Vinson and I looked at each other in silent agreement, recalling the bogus statements about Los Serpientes bringing drugs to the prison. We didn't say it in front of everybody in the tent, but we figured the Warden didn't buy that lie either. With that, the Warden told us not to tell the agents that he planted his own mole to investigate them. We swore ourselves to secrecy. The Warden told us when our next meeting was and then he changed the subject altogether.

Finally, the Warden called Sergeant Thomas on the radio and told him to bring Cobra in to meet us. The Warden suggested that none of the committee members, except the chaplains, speak directly to Cobra because he didn't want Cobra to think he could casually approach any of us publicly. That would create a false impression for the other inmates if they ever saw him speaking to any one of us. The second thing the Warden did was to dismiss all the committee members who were actually guards or officers employed by the prison. He certainly didn't want Cobra to know which prison officers were on any of the committees. That way, he would never know whom he could possibly bribe. By the time the

Warden was finished, the only committee members left in the room to meet this man was Dr. Vinson, me, and the chaplains. Dr. Vinson decided to take the lead and shifted his feet from underneath the table, crossed his legs, folded his arms, and told the Warden to let him in. Alas, we came face to face with the enigmatic monster they call Cobra.

The heavy flap over the doorway of the tent was thrown back and in walked five feet ten inches worth of hostile, tattooed, Hispanic confusion. I took one thorough look at him from head to toe and thought to myself, "My God, this man doesn't need to be in a prison. He needs to be in a straitjacket." It was early in the morning, so all the flaps that covered the openings that were cut into the tent fabric for windows were raised so as much light could enter the tent as possible. All the light allowed us to see the full extent of Cobra's appearance. Oddly enough, all of Los Serpientes' members rolled their sleeves up a certain way to distinguish themselves from other inmates, as if their trademark torture before murder practice wasn't sufficient. But they also cuffed their pants with the cuffs going inward or underneath the bottom of their pants legs and secured them with rubber bands, bread wrappers, or long pieces of thread so their pants legs resembled the pants legs of a soldier wearing boot blousers, and they refused to wear athletic shoes, making them the only inmates on the compound to wear black work boots all year round. So here, sitting before us, was a demented but well-regarded gang member wearing a neatly pressed canary-yellow jumpsuit with the sleeves rolled up and the pants legs cuffed and bound, spit-shined black work boots, a utility worker's tool belt with a yellow hard hat and work gloves hanging from the tool belt, and he was literally draped with hundreds of tattoos that run the gamut.

I couldn't help but stare at the man in utter bewilderment. As best I could tell, he couldn't have been more than thirty to thirty-five years old, and he probably didn't weigh much more than 160 pounds fully dressed and soaking wet, but this was the man currently controlling the most vicious prison gang in North America. I had heard so many bad things about this man that I was actually disappointed when I finally met him because, other than sheer weirdness, there was nothing impressive about him. Dr. Vinson must have had the same opinion because after Cobra sat down and we moved beyond the obvious fact that canary yellow jumpsuits and tattoos aren't really fashionable and shouldn't be paired together, he looked at me and then looked back at Cobra as if to ask, "Is this it?"

No matter what we thought, we remained seated and silent to oblige the Warden, who gave Cobra a little speech of commendation and then shook his hand. When Cobra suspiciously extended his hand to the Warden to receive his handshake, he acknowledged the Warden's praise with a dry, "Thank you." Dr. Vinson and I were both taken aback when

Cobra responded because we noticed his teeth, which appeared to be filed down like fangs. Dr. Vinson gave me a subtle nudge under the table and then motioned for one of the chaplains to ask Cobra an offhand question just so we could see his teeth again when he answered. We both wanted to be certain we saw fangs. I tried to force myself to focus on looking Cobra in his eyes when he answered because I didn't want him, in particular, to be offended by seeing me staring at his teeth when he spoke, but it was impossible. He actually had filed his teeth down to fangs, which convinced me all the more that he was suffering from psychosis or some other kind of pathological delusion, and from that moment on, I wasn't alarmed by Cobra anymore. I really felt sorry for him and wondered what happened in his childhood that caused him to become the monstrosity we were looking at in that tent.

The Warden, slowly pacing back and forth with his hands behind his back, dragged his speech on, including the part about Cobra having weak links in his organization. As the Warden continued speaking, the look on Cobra's face suggested he already knew the Warden was going to tell him he was under surveillance and would be searched on a regular basis, and if perchance any opportunity arose for the Warden to put him in solitary confinement, add more time to his already lengthy sentence, or send him away, he would not hesitate. To add insult to injury, the Warden deliberately spent another ten to fifteen minutes hammering the same points about the snitches bringing information, and if any of it was found to be true, Cobra could expect to receive the maximum punishment, and if he didn't like it, he could write his local congressman. The Warden also drove the point home that Cobra and his gang affiliates at the campsite would be randomly but thoroughly searched without notice and without regard for where they were or what they were presently doing.

Cobra endured the Warden's speech but was no less agitated by the redundant hammering. The Warden dragged this out a few minutes more and then finally brought things to a close by asking Cobra if he had any questions. Cobra didn't say a word. He just stared into space, sucking his filed teeth with his tattooed arms folded and his shaved head cocked to the side. The Warden told Sergeant Thomas to escort Cobra back to wherever he came from, so they both got up and walked out of the tent. After they left, the chaplains, Dr. Vinson, and I made small talk with the Warden for a few minutes. The chaplains hadn't really conversed with us since the argument they had with Dr. Vinson in one of our meetings back on the prison compound. They attended all the meetings after that one, but they usually acted aloof and kept their comments to a minimum. I suppose seeing Cobra struck a nerve and made them feel like talking. We needed to talk anyway because there were far too many inmates and too few staff members at this campsite for us to be at odds with each other.

Our conversation lasted a few minutes, but I gradually brought everybody's attention back to the subject about the college classes for the inmates. This was really a critical situation because although I was setting up the class schedule to coincide with the inmates' work schedules, nobody had really thought about where the classes would, could, or should be held at the campsite. So far, the only tents not being slept in were the tents on the perimeter of the camp where the contracted security teams operated, and those tents were off limits to inmates. So how were we going to pull this off if we didn't have a classroom?

One of the chaplains suggested we use the dining pavilions for class. It sounded good, but we weren't sure we could really implement that idea though because there were only four dining pavilions: one for each group. If we used one of the dining pavilions for class, we would have to split up the dining traffic from that pavilion into three even groups, so there would be an equal number of inmates using the three remaining dining pavilions, but this was easy. The difficult part was figuring out how much more time we would need to allot for the displaced inmates to eat breakfast, lunch, and dinner without interfering with their work schedules or unfairly making them give up sleep or leisure time because they had to use another dining pavilion farther away from where they were camping. The Warden didn't really have a lot of time to talk about it but told me to make the class schedules anyway, and we would find a suitable location for a classroom when he came back from his meeting with the governor. In the meantime, the Warden told me I was free to peruse the entire camp to see where I wanted to set up a tent or something to facilitate the classes. Shortly thereafter, the Warden left us to attend his meeting with the governor.

Dr. Vinson and I stayed a little while, talking to the chaplains about the FBI agents, the Warden's mole, and Cobra for the sake of exchanging thoughts. For the first time in many meetings, we finally agreed that something was really shaky about the FBI, and it left us feeling vulnerable and unsettled. Surprisingly, Chaplain Beasley told us he vaguely remembered working indirectly with one of the undercover FBI agents we're colluding with, but something went wrong during that operation, and an agent was killed. He couldn't remember all the details about who did what or why, but he said he was going to call an old friend of his who worked with him at the time the event happened because if he remembered correctly, the guilty agent was investigated, suspended, and then demoted and reassigned. Chaplain Beasley believed that agent was one of the seven working undercover for us currently, but wasn't quite sure, which is why he never mentioned it before. Dr. Vinson and I both agreed that if that were indeed true, it would explain some of the fictitious information we had received, but until Chaplain Beasley could prove his suspicions, we would let the matter rest. Since Dr. Vinson and I had some extra time on our hands, we bid the chaplains farewell and went back to investigate the clearing we stumbled across earlier.

On our way back to the clearing, we decided to take a short detour to the mobile commissary in that sector of the camp. Dr. Vinson wanted to buy a couple of toothbrushes, so we could brush away excess dirt from anything of interest we found. He also decided to use the bag the clerk at the commissary gave him to collect and disguise whatever we found. That way, if anybody saw us, they would simply think he bought something small from the commissary. Incidentally, we took a few toothpicks from the mobile kitchen trailer also to use on our mini expedition. Off we went back into the woods to the clearing to try to gather as many clues as we could about what happened in that area. On our first trip, we arrived at the clearing from the southern end of the camp going straight south. This time, we decided to go to the clearing from the southeastern part of the camp to see if maybe some artifacts were left behind that would tell the story about what happened in that area.

The brush on the eastern side of the camp was still quite thick, and none of the slope stakes had been hammered into the ground yet because apparently that side of the camp still needed to be surveyed. This area was so heavily wooded that they couldn't survey it until they actually cut some of the trees down first. Dr. Vinson thought it was a safer approach because no one could see us in the thicket so we couldn't be followed, but if someone did try to follow us, we now had an alternate route to and from the clearing. Thus, we slowly worked our way through the brush, moving one step at a time crossing over poison ivy, oak, and sumac plants along the ground. We were also trying to avoid being pricked by the thistles in the weeds that were packed tightly all around us. Thank God I was wearing pants and a long sleeve shirt; otherwise, I would have been badly scratched and scraped by all the bushes. I don't know what Dr. Vinson was expecting to find in all of this, but I didn't see how it was possible to identify something unless it hit us in the face because the thicket was just too dense, and I was moving as fast as I could to get out of it.

After what seemed like an eternity in the woods, we reached the southeastern side of the clearing, and to my surprise, it really did look different and there appeared to be an entirely different story being told from that vantage point. Before we actually stepped into the cleared area, Dr. Vinson suggested we look for any signs of disturbance in the topography like trails, holes, or uneven surfaces that couldn't have been made by animals or Mother Nature. With that in mind, I started looking for variations in land elevation, hoping something would stand out and become noticeable. I didn't see any obvious man-made holes or trails, but I did notice some small, obscure, shiny stones on the ground.

Perhaps they weren't stones, but they looked as if they had been polished and they were oddly shaped. I decided not to touch anything because I didn't know what I was touching and I didn't want to disturb the findings, so I called Dr. Vinson to come and have a look at the stone-like objects on the ground. He pulled out a small magnifying glass first and then scooped up the stones and dropped them in his commissary bag. I asked him if he knew what the stones actually were. He said he had an idea but wanted to look around a little longer for concrete evidence before he gave his opinion.

We kept searching the area on the perimeter of the clearing for clues but found none, so we decided to step back into the woods to continue our search but only a few feet into the woods this time. We moved from the southeastern end all the way around to the western side of the clearing, and it was there that our search unearthed some priceless artifacts that would enlighten us about the area. Dr. Vinson found what appeared to be an ancient sharpened stone used for cutting or chopping like an ax. We also found several more of those polished pebbles, but our most significant find was just a tad bit further into the woods on the southwestern side of the clearing, which was literally behind it. When we started examining that area, we saw some medium-sized mounds on the ground that at a distance could easily have been mistaken for prairie dog mounds, so we moved closer to them for a better view. Naturally, this area was overgrown with weeds and shrub native to wooded areas, so the mounds were completely covered with vegetation. We didn't have any shovels to dig through the mounds, not that we thought we should've anyway, and Dr. Vinson was convinced we shouldn't disturb them at all until we had a better idea of what could possibly have been placed underneath the mounds, so we searched around the mounds to gain answers.

There were probably ten to twelve mounds in all on that side of the clearing, and they didn't seem symmetrical in size and weren't necessarily dug in straight rows either. They were just there, random casual things that showed up at different times and needed to be covered, but somehow, the spot they wanted was taken. Since it wasn't a planned arrival, they just picked another spot and piled dirt upon themselves. Of course, that's an unfounded surface hypothesis fitting for a novice explorer. However, an excavation of the area would be the best solution, but the government wasn't about to turn their immigration zone into a science project simply because there were mounds behind our camp. Something far greater would have to happen for them to send a team of scientific explorers into the area to conduct research, so Dr. Vinson and I continued searching to see if there was something greater or worth reporting.

Aside from the mounds, the cutting stone, and the shiny pebbles, it seemed as if we had reached the apex of our exploration, and the results were just going to be our own secret. We started walking through the brush heading southeast in the direction that we arrived in, and something on the ground drew Dr. Vinson's attention. I stopped just behind him and asked him what he was looking at while I visibly searched behind and around us to make sure no one else was in the woods. Dr. Vinson didn't speak, so I asked the same question a second time. He still didn't speak. I came from behind him and stood next to him to see what he saw that rendered him speechless. I gently took his arm and asked him if he was okay, and there was long sigh and pause before he finally answered me. He said he knew what the clearing was used for and what the mounds and shiny pebbles were. I stood there silently and waited for him to tell me what it was, but he didn't readily offer the answer, so I asked again if he was okay. He turned towards me at the moment and asked me if I could remember the last time I went to a child's funeral? I stood there with a blank look on my face, trying to associate the question to the present moment, and then it dawned on me what he was trying to say about the clearing.

Dr. Vinson gathered himself and said rather frankly that we shouldn't dig in that area because the clearing was a killing ground where the former natives offered human sacrifices of children. The bodies were cut up with sharp stones like the one we found and offered to their gods. After the sacrifice was made, the blood was drained from the body, which explained in part why nothing was growing on the ground in that area; the body parts were then piled up and dirt thrown on top of them. That's what the mounds are, and the shiny pebbles we found were actually human teeth that were polished and also offered as some kind of oblation. I asked him how he was able to deduce all of that without digging up the mounds or being able to thoroughly inspect the area with a scientific research team. He pointed to the right, and there was a mound that didn't have as much dirt, but it was no less a mound. It had been weather-beaten, and years of environmental changes had blown whatever dirt used, if any, away. So it was just a mound of human bones with grass and other weeds growing around and through the pile that only God knows how long had been there. It was quite obvious the bones belonged to children because they were so small. In fact, the skulls looked like they could've once belonged to a child so young that it wasn't walking yet.

CHAPTER SEVEN

Dr. Vinson stood there, sweating and lost for words, trying to recall what kind of culture would've offered up its children to idols in that area. I was completely speechless, but my mind was moving at the speed of light trying to configure a face I had never seen before to the shape of the little skulls thrown on that pile like useless garbage. I imagined small children, innocent children, and happy children running, playing, laughing, and being children who were unknowingly bred for slaughter. I wondered if their god was ever appeased when their blood was drained and bodies ripped apart like animal flesh. I wondered if their mothers' cried when they found out they were pregnant, knowing there was always a possibility that their child would be sacrificed. I wondered if the family was permitted to mourn the loss of their sister or brother, nephew or niece, cousin, or son or daughter. I wondered if a monetary value could have been placed upon a child's life. If it could, I wondered if that child or those children could have been bought at an auction to spare them from being sacrificed for a god that didn't love them enough to provide his own sacrificial ram in a bush nearby.

Dr. Vinson took off his glasses and rubbed the sweat from his forehead with his right forearm. He didn't look at me, but he said rather firmly that we needed to go back to the camp and inform the Warden and others about this area before we started digging and unearthing things that didn't need to be disturbed. I fully agreed, and we started moving with a purpose like soldiers marching to war. We had to walk back through the woods in the thick brush, but it didn't seem to take as long on the way back as did when we arrived. We walked completely around the clearing from the western side to the northern side, which placed us on the southern perimeter of the camp again. This was how we initially found the clearing to begin with. We kept walking until we saw the slope stakes, the tree markers, and the pond with the small fish and tadpoles, and then we reached the edge of the campsite where Sergeant Thomas happened to be standing with his back to us, yelling and swearing at the top of his lungs at some inmates for something.

We saw Sergeant Thomas, but we didn't see Sergeant Thomas. We saw him with our eyes, but our minds were far from him, so we walked completely around him and the degraded inmates without stopping. Since we walked around him and never stopped to acknowledge him, he ceased yelling at the inmates and asked us where had we been and where were we going. We kept moving without speaking, and, apparently, it offended him because he ran in front of us and cut off our path.

Dr. Vinson politely warned him to move because our business was urgent, but Sergeant Thomas didn't move. Dr. Vinson and I tried to move to the right, but Sergeant Thomas wouldn't let us pass. We tried to move to the left and he cut us off again. Meanwhile, he perceived this as a rare moment for him to reiterate his "disrespected black man" speech to me, so he continued impeding our progress by moving right when we moved right and moving left when we moved left, rehearsing his disgust for me and other black women he felt didn't respect him all the while. I wasn't emotionally engaged in Sergeant Thomas's comments at the moment so I simply told him that I would deal with him some other time and pressed forward, but he wouldn't let it go.

I had dealt with Sergeant Thomas and many other males similar to him before, especially at the prison. I knew the quickest way to end his show was to let him rant to himself and not respond, so I remained silent while he yapped on about why I was wrong for this and that. On the contrary, Dr. Vinson's patience was worn thin and he was extremely annoyed by Sergeant Thomas, so much that he initiated an entirely new conversation with me during Sergeant Thomas's monologue so we could both ignore him. Now as long as we were on the compound, Sergeant Thomas knew his limitations and never touched me. There were too many other staff members, too many inmates, and too many cameras all over the compound in every crack and crevice of that unit. Since we were outside in a wide open campsite with no cameras and the inmates and staff members were scattered all over the place, he thought he had the liberty to put his hands on me, so he grabbed my left arm while yelling in my face that he wasn't finished talking to me yet. Immediately, something inside me triggered a set of thoughts and emotions that can be best characterized by the word, "offense," and I felt my nostrils flare and my lips tighten. I could feel blood rapidly rushing through my body. My breaths became heavy, deep, and short; the pulse in my neck beat so hard, it felt like someone was thumping me. I felt the muscles in my forehead pull my eyebrows down such that my upbeat countenance now became a highly indented frown fueled by years of unrequited respect.

From the moment I began working at the prison, Sergeant Thomas has willfully and openly antagonized me, and I have done all that I could do to avoid saying the things I really wanted to say, knowing they would emasculate him. For years, I have been treading lightly around certain subjects and issues regarding him in an effort to avoid taking part in malicious gossip, and I refused to stoop to his level and dignify his idiotic behavior. Unlike himself, he fails to realize that I don't feel empowered by knowing or possessing hurtful information about other people. In fact, I actually wish I didn't know embarrassing things about him but I do, and each time he comes to me with his black man nonsense, I am tempted to pull those degrading skeletons out of the closet in my mind and throw them at him publicly.

Often, I have tried to engage him in a mature and intelligent manner, but each attempt usually resulted in an unproductive one-sided conversation that he used as a platform to criticize my success and attack me as a black woman who views him as just another man. Aside from the fact that he is obnoxious and casually sleeps with several women at the same time, he is simply not my type. Even if he was a soft-spoken, celibate college graduate, I still wouldn't go out with him and he refuses to accept that. But none of that really matters presently. What matters is that he has his hands on me, and they are about to be removed by any means necessary.

I saw Sergeant Thomas's lips moving, but I didn't hear much of what he said because my attention was focused on his right hand, which was tightly wrapped around my left arm, and his left index finger was moving up and down in front of my face a few inches from my nose. In a matter of seconds, I graduated from being irritated to being enraged by Sergeant Thomas's audacity to grab me. I know better than anyone that I am a woman, but I have never considered myself susceptible to violence, especially from a co-worker, just because I work in a prison. I had completely tuned him out while I stood there, occupied with prying his fingers from around my arm. Dr. Vinson was also yelling for him to let me go, but instead I felt his grip tighten around my arm. Finally, the natural instincts that take over when someone feels threatened kicked in, and before I knew it I had my drawn my firearm and placed the barrel of my handgun on the bridge of his nose. Immediately, everyone stopped moving and speaking and there was dead silence.

I looked Sergeant Thomas in the eyes without wavering or flinching and calmly told him to let me go and leave me alone. I thought perhaps he might have been in shock, especially since there was a loaded pistol pressed against the flesh between his eyes, because he didn't move right away. Maybe he thought I was joking and he was going to call my bluff. Whatever he was thinking, he only had seconds to decide because I wasn't going through this with him anymore. I did eventually feel his grip loosen a bit, although he still had his hand around my arm, but he wasn't moving fast enough for me. So I released the safety, moved the hammer back, and without wavering or flinching, looked him squarely in the eye and calmly told him again to let me go and leave me alone. I could see the pupils in his eyes get smaller as he as looked back and forth at the weapon in his face and me, so I knew he understood.

The faint sound of Dr. Vinson calling me by my first name began to register as Sergeant Thomas gradually released my arm and stepped backward. Our eyes were still fixed on each other, slowly measuring each precarious movement one motion at a time. There is something about the sound of an armed weapon being detonated that moves people to act in accordance with the gunman's wishes. But it should never have come to this. Unfortunately, the only language Sergeant Thomas speaks is one that involves threatening others to get results because that is all he knows in the prison world, but I am neither an inmate nor am I one of his whores. He does not intimidate me either.

Once I lowered my weapon and he was standing a good eleven or twelve feet from me, he put his hands in his pockets and started smirking, saying I wasn't really going to shoot him and every woman has a price. He just hasn't figured out what mine is yet. I hadn't put my gun back in the holster yet. I thought that maybe I should shoot at him just for being the jerk he was, but I could actually feel Dr. Vinson tugging on my right arm now so we could do what we had originally set out to do. Instead, I put my weapon away and we started walking toward the main control unit. As soon as we turned around, I heard footsteps running toward me. Dr. Vinson and I both turned around quickly, and Sergeant Thomas was running toward me with his fists balled up to punch me.

When he got within striking distance, he swung at me, cursing and yelling that no woman talks to him that way and that he was going to teach me a lesson. I aimed my weapon at him and told him to stop but he refused. I was flabbergasted! I felt I was bending over backwards now because I had already drawn my weapon once and spared him. Now his blatant disrespect for me escalated to rage, so after he swung the second time, I fired a shot that grazed the left side of his neck just outside the jugular and I told him I wouldn't miss next time. He knew I was an expert shooter who could have killed him at that distance if I wanted to, so he finally took me seriously and provoked me no further. As the blood ran down his neck onto his clothes, his posture and facial expression implied surrender and he walked away. However, the sound of gunfire in the camp set off a chain of events that would have to be intelligently explained. Otherwise, there would be a thorough but unnecessary investigation that might lead to suspension or termination.

The shot rang out throughout the camp, and the inmates were forced into an outdoor lock-down situation until the staff members could find out what happened. Several officers came running in the direction the shot came from. They found us standing there and began trying to piece together what had just happened between Sergeant Thomas and me. I was temporarily in shock.

I could not believe I was going to have to shoot him to make him leave me alone. Meanwhile, Dr. Vinson took off his glasses and began filibustering to give me time to gather myself. But before I could admit I fired the shot, Sergeant Thomas reappeared with a cravat wrapped around his neck, implying he was attacked by a snake hanging from a tree in the woods that he eventually yanked down and shot. He apologized and said the snake caught him off guard and he just instinctively shot it. The officers asked me and Dr. Vinson if what Sergeant Thomas said was true. Dr. Vinson simply pointed at Sergeant Thomas's neck and said the proof was there. They then asked Sergeant Thomas what he was doing in the woods. He looked at Dr. Vinson and me and told the officers he was helping us find our way back to the camp. At that moment, Dr. Vinson took Sergeant Thomas's cue and began explaining in small detail what we found behind the campsite. The officers seemed pacified with the story so they escorted Dr. Vinson and me back to the main control unit and took Sergeant Thomas to the closest outdoor medical facility.

The Warden hadn't come back from his meeting with the governor yet, so Dr. Vinson used the time to contact some of his colleagues for help. He made several phone calls to other anthropologists he knew and had worked with on previous expeditions. He also uploaded the pictures he took of the mounds and bones from his digital camera so they would have something concrete to look at while they were researching the ancient tribes that would have been prevalent in the area where our campsite was. We started reading several cultural websites about human sacrifice, especially the sacrifice of children, that Dr. Vinson had private access to. While we were waiting for feedback from his colleagues, Dr. Vinson got a hit from one the sites about ancient ritual practices.

According to the information he received, we were about to start digging up an area that was previously occupied by tribal communities that believed in human sacrifice or had direct contact with other communities who sacrificed humans to their gods. It was only a preliminary finding though. Researchers would have to come and study the area and extract samples of the bones and other artifacts to make a solid determination. Since this was the issue, Dr. Vinson had to find a way to present this to the Warden, the governor, and whoever else needed to know to see if they would actually care enough to have the area examined. His presentation would have to be rather convincing, especially if he wanted the governor to delay construction on that side of the camp. He hastily started compiling the initial information he retrieved from the websites we were viewing. Some of his colleagues also sent additional information to him that supported his original hypothesis. By the time the Warden came back, Dr. Vinson had a full presentation ready for his listeners.

The Warden arrived with an emissary from the governor's office a little after five o'clock that evening. He looked somewhat distressed, but then again, he always looked a little distressed. He casually introduced the man to us and said he would be inspecting our work on the project for the next seven or eight weeks to make sure everything ran smoothly. Dr. Vinson motioned for the Warden and the governor's emissary, Mr. Townsend, to sit down at the table in the center of the tent. He nonchalantly offered them some coffee and sat down at the table with them. The Warden sensed that something might have been wrong, so he asked Dr. Vinson if there was anything in particular that he needed to tell him. Looking over the rim of his glasses, Dr. Vinson informally stated there was something he needed to discuss with the Warden, and since the governor's emissary was present, he needed to listen, too.

Dr. Vinson told the Warden and Mr. Townsend about our findings behind the southern end of the camp and suggested a small scientific team come in and examine the area as a safety precaution. He showed both of them the presentation he had quickly put together and offered to guide them to the area so they could see it for themselves. The Warden and Mr. Townsend agreed to view the area but decided to change into something more suitable for trekking through the woods. Their suits and wing-tipped shoes were going to be scathed by rocks, thorns, bushes, vines, and a variety of plants growing everywhere. While we eagerly waited for them to get dressed, we decided to pack some flashlights, bottled water, and gloves this time. We knew from our previous trips that the woods would be physically taxing, and we didn't want to get caught out there in the dark without some kind of light either. After about twenty minutes, the Warden and Mr. Townsend came back to the main control unit and we left heading for the clearing.

The Warden asked Dr. Vinson if he had shown anyone else or spoken to anyone else about the clearing. Dr. Vinson responded he had mentioned it earlier to a few of the officers but didn't have a deep discussion about it, and no one had seen his presentation or followed us to the clearing. Mr. Townsend asked us if we had spotted any wild animals in the area. We assured him the area was completely vacant; at least it had been when we were there earlier. We mutely moved at a moderate pace through the woods, allowing the Warden and Mr. Townsend more time to navigate through the brush we were already familiar with. We were all silently conserving as much of our energy as possible for the hike. We came back to the slope stakes and then to the pond with the small fish and the tadpoles, and then on farther until we saw the clearing. When the Warden and Mr. Townsend initially saw the clearing, they had the same reaction Dr. Vinson and I had when we first saw it. They also thought it was unusual that an area would be cleared in the middle of the woods like that. Still, Dr. Vinson trekked on farther, guiding us around to the western side of the clearing. Finally, he stopped when he saw the mounds, and the Warden and Mr. Townsend beheld the area, the bones, and the shiny human teeth on the ground.

The Warden and Mr. Townsend stepped tentatively through the area with respect to what they might see or step on. Mr. Townsend pulled out his own camera and snapped several pictures of the bones protruding from the mound and the shiny teeth. The Warden asked Dr. Vinson if he had already taken some of the teeth for observation because he wanted to gather some of the teeth for himself, but not as souvenirs. Dr. Vinson told both the Warden and Mr. Townsend that they could collect teeth and other smaller objects that lay loosely on the ground, but the mounds and bones were not to be disturbed. They agreed and only gathered other objects that looked like pottery fragments or other kinds of handmade items from the ground and took more pictures. When they were satisfied, we left the area and went back to the camp.

Once inside, Mr. Townsend called the governor's office, explaining what he had seen and heard about the clearing. He asked the governor if he objected to having that area thoroughly examined before they cleared it altogether for the project. The governor said it was the Warden's project site and he could handle it as he saw fit as long as construction on the other areas began on time. The Warden asked Dr. Vinson if he personally knew some experts in his line of work that would take on such a project on short notice without contracted pay. Dr. Vinson told the Warden he had already been in touch with some of his colleagues who would be grateful just to get out of their stuffy university offices. Moreover, they were tenured professors who were highly paid for their expertise, so not being paid for this project wasn't going to be an issue. The matter now settled, the Warden told the governor the rest of the project would commence as scheduled but he would have this area checked before they dug it up. At the very least, he wanted ensure they weren't desecrating something culturally important to the future residents of this area.

Since this was Sunday evening, we had one more committee meeting before the work began tomorrow morning at eight o'clock. The Warden told Dr. Vinson to make his presentation tonight at the meeting so he could inform the others about what was going to be happening over the next few weeks. They also needed to know because now we were going to have to rotate working as security to accompany the researchers who would be working among us. It was really a menial job that gave us some extra time to sit around, read, listen to music, or toy with our computers. I, on the other hand, wouldn't be able to personally accompany the researchers because I had classes to teach that would be starting in another week. My schedule was booked because of teaching, grading papers, and performing the other tasks I was already selected to perform at the camp. I would be lucky if I could just gather small details from the researchers over lunch. I didn't feel slighted by it though because I knew Dr. Vinson was going to tell me everything he could about what they found. So I set the matter to rest, gathered my things from the tent, and Dr. Vinson and I went to the dining pavilion for dinner.

I was hungry and not hungry at the same time. The food looked delicious, but I was really concerned about what we had stumbled upon today so my appetite was a little sketchy. I didn't ask Dr. Vinson these questions, but I was thinking, "What were we really getting ourselves into and why had no one examined this area before we got here?" It just all seemed so strange to me that this wasn't already done, but I suppose people generally don't think about who may have died on a plot of land before they buy and cultivate it. They just focus on what they want to do with it now. So I sat there slightly melancholy, raking my fork through my corn, when Dr. Vinson finally broke the silence and asked me how I felt about the whole Sergeant Thomas issue.

I couldn't answer right away because I had honestly put it out of my mind for a while. All the excitement about the clearing had completely taken over everything else that had happened today. I had to think about it all over again to respond, but even then I don't think I gave him an honest answer. I didn't lie. It's just that I wasn't in the heat of that moment anymore, so what I may have felt then I didn't feel now. I think he asked me though because he thought it might have hurt my feelings as a woman to be forced into shooting at Sergeant Thomas. He knows I'm not a violent person, and I would exhaust all my diplomatic resources to prevent violence that could be prevented. But Sergeant Thomas left me no choice so it didn't hurt my feelings to shoot at him; it just made mad, and there is a huge difference between being hurt and being angry.

We toyed with our dinner a little longer, picking only select pieces of meat and veggies to eat as small children would. I asked Dr. Vinson what time his friends would arrive tomorrow to start examining the area. He said some of them were so glad to leave their campuses, they would be flying in late tonight; others would show up tomorrow around six o'clock in the morning, ready for work. He said they usually only went on long, laborious expeditions that occurred periodically, depending on the cost. Everything they researched in the name of the university had to be formally approved and fully funded. Since this was personal, they all jumped at the opportunity to see something different. I asked him if he needed me to do anything in particular to help with the presentation later on during the meeting. He took his glasses off, rubbed his eyes, and stated that everything he wanted to say was already in order, but he did need help setting up the slide show on the projector, so I agreed to operate the computer to forward his slides. The meeting wasn't for another hour and a half, so we sat in the dining pavilion another thirty minutes or so and then left to relax before the meeting.

We went back to my tent and I plopped down on my cot with my legs extended over the end and my head settled on two pillows. I actually had two cots in the tent and an air mattress that was still in the box, but I was the only person occupying the tent. I had been expecting another professor, but she didn't show up. I didn't want to be too hasty and spread all my stuff out on both sides of the tent in case they assigned someone else to stay. I kept my things neatly compartmentalized under, around, and next to my cot for the time being. Dr. Vinson came in behind me and flung himself down on the empty cot across from me. He kicked his shoes off and breathed a long sigh. A few minutes later, he was snoring. I set my alarm to go off before the meeting was supposed to start so we could refresh ourselves with a cup of hot tea after a short nap. I got up quickly before I drifted off and lit two generic candles on my desk. I pulled the tent door flap down and lay back down on my cot. I kicked my shoes off and a few minutes later I drifted off to sleep.

It was déjà vu with a twist. I was dreaming that Dr. Vinson and I needed to come back to the camp so we could tell the Warden about the clearing all over again. We walked around the western part of the clearing to the northern part. We kept walking north until we saw the slope stakes, the little pond with the small fish and the tadpoles, and finally the southern end of the camp where Sergeant Thomas was standing with two inmates he was yelling at for unknown reasons. We walked completely around them without interrupting them, but Sergeant Thomas was offended because we didn't stop and speak to him. He ran ahead of us and cut off our path, demanding we tell him where we had been and where we were going. Dr. Vinson brushed him off and told him to move because we had urgent business with the Warden. Sergeant Thomas grabbed my left arm with his right hand and started wagging the index finger on his left hand in front of my face, yelling and swearing all the while that he wasn't finished talking to me yet.

Just like the first time, I tried to pry his fingers from my arm, but he tightened his grip and wouldn't let me go. His lips were moving, but I couldn't hear what he was saying. I saw Dr. Vinson grab Sergeant Thomas's left arm, trying to get him to release me, but the more Dr. Vinson tried, the tighter Sergeant Thomas's grip became around my arm. I drew my weapon, released the safety, let the hammer back, and aimed right between Sergeant Thomas's eyes. He finally let me go, but he was angrier now than he was before because I pulled my gun on him. He cautiously backed up a few feet then lunged forward and swung at me with his fist, so I fired a shot. This time, the bullet went through the left side of Sergeant Thomas's neck, and he fell down on the ground bleeding.

Discombobulated, Dr. Vinson and I stood over him while he gasped for air, fighting to keep his spirit inside his body. The stream of dark red blood gushed from his neck, settling on the ground under his head and got bigger and bigger with each breath he fought to take. As he squirmed on the ground with one foot in the present and one foot in eternity, he reached up to us for help and used one of his last few breaths to wheeze out a faint, "I'm sorry." Dr. Vinson called for help on his radio, but before help could arrive, Sergeant Thomas's struggle for life ended. I had killed him. I had killed him and I knew he was dead because I could smell something living leave his body when he stopped breathing. The blood kept seeping out of the wound on his neck until the blood was just about gone. He lay motionless on the ground in his hard-hat and overalls, covered with dirt and beads of sweat. We stood there looking at him, not really knowing what to say or how we should feel about him because he had taken this situation too far. It was almost as if he wanted me to shoot him. Why didn't he just stop? Why did he grab me in the first place? Who did he think he was to put his hands on me?

Dr. Vinson tried to assure me everything was going to turn out fine because he was going to give a statement on my behalf suggesting the shooting happened strictly in self-defense. I wasn't sure Dr. Vinson's statement would be credible — though it was true — because every-body knows we have a close friendship. They might think he was lying to cover up something for me. There were two inmates close by also, but I didn't know how much of the incident they saw. Even if they did see it all, they would undoubtedly use it to leverage some kind of deal for themselves. I didn't have a game plan for this situation, so I just decided to tell the truth with the hope it would be enough. That being said, Dr. Vinson knelt down over Sergeant Thomas's body, placing his index finger and middle finger on his eyelids and pulled them down. Sergeant Thomas was dead, but his eyes were still open. When Dr. Vinson stood up, Sergeant Thomas opened his eyes, gasping for air. My alarm went off.

I lifted my body up off my cot, startled by Sergeant Thomas and by my alarm. It was 7:00 PM and the meeting was starting in fifty minutes. I realized then I hadn't seen Sergeant Thomas since the incident. In fact, no one had really seen him since he left the infirmary, but no one asked about him either. Maybe that was the reason why he put so much effort into getting peoples' attention; he didn't feel appreciated. I made two small cups of tea and gave one to Dr. Vinson, who was struggling to sit upright and put his shoes on at the edge of the cot. I told him I had a bad dream and was disturbed by what happened with Sergeant Thomas today. I wanted to talk to him after the meeting if he was willing. I did-n't really know what I was going to say, but I knew I couldn't let things go on the way they had gone so far. Dr. Vinson asked me if I wanted him to be there just to ensure he wasn't going to grab me again, but I told him I felt pretty confident this would go smoothly and declined his offer. We sipped tea silently in preparation for the meeting until 7:50 PM and then we left my tent.

When we arrived for the meeting, all the committee members,

including the chaplains, were anxious to hear about the clearing. Gossip had already circulated about the area, but no one knew for sure except me, Dr. Vinson, the Warden, and Mr. Townsend. The Warden introduced Mr. Townsend and talked about the governor's expectations with this project. Mr. Townsend then stood and gave a brief overview of what was going to happen starting tomorrow and explained his responsibility to inspect our project site for code compliance reasons. They both made a few other general comments and then turned the meeting over to Dr. Vinson. I began the slide show and dimmed the lights. Everybody focused his or her attention on Dr. Vinson, but I noticed that Sergeant Thomas wasn't there. He wasn't a committee member, but he was the Warden's right-hand man who had unlimited access to just about everything. I decided after the meeting I would find him and apologize to him for what happened today. I didn't think it was my fault, but I felt like the dream was a sign that he really needed help but just didn't know how to ask. Besides, if we were going to bury this hatchet, we had to start somewhere.

CHAPTER EIGHT

The dozers, front-end loaders, and dump trucks were cranked up at six o'clock this morning. The smell of fresh diesel filled the air, and everybody was eager to start working on the project today. We had an informal semi-ribbon cutting ceremony spearheaded by Mr. Townsend before the first tree was knocked down and cleared. Shortly thereafter, the inmates were platooned by the color of their overalls and marched to their respective work areas. Saws were buzzing, hammers were pounding, and the dump trucks were lined up, waiting to be filled with dirt, boulders and smaller rocks, debris, and anything else on the ground that couldn't be used to build. I stood gazing at the herds of inmates moving north, east, and west in unison on the project site and it was beautiful. I only wished the people who had written off these inmates and considered them savages that couldn't be civilized could see what they were doing.

Dr. Vinson caught me by surprise and gently placed his hand on my shoulder to get my attention. The roar from the heavy equipment was loud; we practically had to yell to hear each other talk unless we walked toward the perimeter of the camp away from the equipment. He introduced me to his professional colleagues who had come to research the clearing: Dr. Harvard, Dr. Princeton, and Dr. Yale. They arrived late last night, but there were two others who would be joining them later today: Dr. Brown and Dr. Cornell. They were all quite charming and distinguished-looking gentlemen who wore tweed sports coats, loafers, and khaki pants, much like Dr. Vinson. Dr. Harvard and Dr. Yale had noticeable British accents, and Dr. Princeton had an accent exclusive to his home in Sydney, Australia. They all seemed to have a pleasant sense of humor and were excited to be working at our campsite. I accompanied them to the main control unit where we met up with the Warden and Mr. Townsend.

Dr. Vinson introduced his friends to the Warden and Mr. Townsend, who agreed to give them an official tour of the entire site. They all shook hands, grabbed some bottles of water from the refrigerator, and left for the tour. While they were out, Dr. Vinson stayed behind and asked me to help him set up some additional computers and lab equipment his colleagues brought with them to start testing the samples he had already retrieved from the clearing. The Warden agreed to have an additional tent set up next to the main control unit for the scientists to perform their work in. We arranged the tables, computers, microscopes, special lights, and other equipment they brought to simulate an outdoor lab for them. After we finished, we sat down a few minutes to talk, and I asked Dr. Vinson if he had seen Sergeant Thomas. He said he hadn't seen him but thought I had talked to him after the meeting last night. I told him I didn't have the opportunity to speak with Sergeant Thomas because he didn't show up for the meeting. We both acknowledged it was not like him to miss a meeting but decided to casually look for him on our own before we asked anyone else about his whereabouts.

The Warden brought the scientists back. We could hear them next door in the other tent discussing the particulars of how they were going to conduct their research and what they had to do if they found something that would cause the project to be aborted on the southern side of the camp. Mr. Townsend told them they could not release information to anyone under any circumstances unless the governor permitted them to do so. They agreed to keep their findings contained but asked Mr. Townsend if the governor had any safety measures in place for something of this nature. They wanted to know specifically if the governor was prepared in case they discovered something eminently dangerous. What was the protocol if it turned out they were dealing with a serial killer or some wild animals that eat people?

The Warden told them they would be accompanied at all times by armed staff members who also carried radios. If they had contact with any wild animals, there was a national park nearby where the animals would be safely transported and released back into the wild. However, if they had contact with any humans who were not associated with this project, including illegal aliens crossing the border, the staff members were to shoot them without question. The scientists sat silently, waiting for the Warden to tell them there was an alternative to shooting the unknown humans, but there was none. One of them spoke for the group and told the Warden they understood clearly what was to happen and thanked him for the tour, then they all left and went back to their living quarters to change and start working.

Dr. Vinson and I waited for the group of scientists in their work tent while they were changing clothes. We were going to take them to the clearing to gather more artifacts for their research. While we were putting the finishing touches on the lab, we heard Sergeant Thomas's voice just outside the tent. I walked swiftly out of the tent to meet him so we could finally talk about what happened yesterday. He had a few inmates with him that were assigned to some work detail he was in charge of, so I stood there and waited for him to finish giving the inmates their instructions. After the inmates left, I said, "Good morning," but he ignored me and started walking away. I called his name twice, but he acted like he didn't hear me and kept walking. I caught up with him and told him we needed to talk about what happened so we could have closure. He called me the "B" word and told me to stay away from him and leave him alone. Otherwise, he would shoot at me the way I shot at him. I told him he provoked me to shoot at him because he grabbed me and then he threw a punch at me. He said he threw a punch at me because I had no business walking away from him when he was talking and that I needed to be brought down a notch because I didn't know my place as a woman. That was all the closure I needed. The conversation ended there and I never thought about it anymore.

I went back to the tent, and Dr. Vinson and the scientists were waiting for me so we could head out for the clearing. I grabbed my gloves and a bottle of water while we informally conversed about Mr. Townsend and the Warden. The scientists were a little distressed with the command to shoot all unidentified humans, knowing we were close to the border and the likelihood of seeing an illegal alien was high. What was the point in constructing a resettlement zone if we were going to kill some of the futures residents for it? Dr. Vinson and I both agreed some of the policies we had to live by seemed extreme, but we also let the scientists know those extreme policies were there for our protection. We made it plain to them that in this world you don't get a second chance to make a first impression, and if the inmates know you're afraid of them, they won't waste any time taking full advantage of it. Dr. Vinson also assured them the Warden was really a respectable person who had just been hardened by life. He was a highly decorated former Marine who received many medals for his leadership, especially in Vietnam. Military wars and prison life had just made him somewhat of a pessimist, but he had a good heart and could be trusted. The real question was could we trust Mr. Townsend?

We didn't know anything about this man, and nobody had real proof he was even who he said he was. We didn't know if he really worked for the governor or not. He could've been spying for some private company, the FBI, or some other faction for all we knew. The scientists asked us when Mr. Townsend arrived and had we bothered to search his background yet. Dr. Vinson told them he hadn't personally checked Mr. Townsend's background and he didn't know if the Warden had him checked either. All we knew is that the Warden supposedly went to a last-minute unscheduled meeting with the governor Sunday and came back with this man. Dr. Princeton told us we needed to be very careful about how much information we gave Mr. Townsend since we didn't know whom we were dealing with because it was possible his presence was a setup. It was interesting that Dr. Princeton said that and it made me recall a statement by the Warden about having his own mole planted at the campsite. But if Mr. Townsend was the mole, why would the Warden introduce him to us? If it was meant to be a secret, the Warden wouldn't have introduced him to us, unless he was also playing both sides to see who he could really trust. Whatever the case was, this was becoming a complicated situation with undercover players, double agents, and prison espionage, right in the middle of a project site with dead bodies on the horizon.

We arrived at the site and the scientists began shoveling dirt away from the mound with the bones so they could collect them. They filled one knapsack up with dirt so they could find out what kinds of chemicals were in the dirt and a second knapsack with bones to determine the bones' age, the gender of the person they belonged to, the possible age of the person at the time they died, and other important information. They also took samples of the plants in the area and some of the rocks for geological study. After they collected enough samples, we headed back to the camp to their tent so they could work. By the time we got back, the other scientists had arrived from the airport, changed clothes, and were waiting in their makeshift lab for us. Dr. Vinson introduced me to them; they cordially greeted each other and began working. I left them alone for a few hours so I could finish putting the campsite class schedule together because school was starting in one week.

The Warden saw me leave their tent and decided to walk with me while I meandered around the campsite looking for a suitable place to hold the classes. I welcomed the company, and we talked about the weather, the progress we were making today, and other generic things. He eventually got around to asking me how everything was going and did I have any problems with anyone in particular. I knew right then that he had heard something about what happened between Sergeant Thomas and me. I was compelled to tell him everything so I wouldn't feel as if I was hiding something. When I finished, the Warden told me he appreciated my honesty but admitted he already knew. He said one of the inmates with Sergeant Thomas at the time of the incident told him everything because Sergeant Thomas later tried to take his anger out on him and the other inmate with them by instigating a fight. Together, they got the best of Sergeant Thomas, and he had to go back to the infirmary later the previous night. The inmates didn't want to serve any more time than they are currently serving so they spilled their guts about it all.

I told the Warden I tried to speak to Sergeant Thomas earlier today so we could resolve the issue once and for all, but Sergeant Thomas blew me off. The Warden told me to just let it go. He said Sergeant Thomas is a good officer, and he has tried to reason with him about his attitude for years. He just doesn't listen. Regardless, he needs to know this kind of behavior is unacceptable. The Warden said Sergeant Thomas wasn't going to speak to me because he's mad about his suspension, but it was his own fault and he would have been fired already if the Warden didn't need him so much. Consequently, the Warden apologized to me and told me if anything like that ever happened again, he would put a bullet in

Sergeant Thomas himself. I felt relieved the Warden knew about it, but I felt bad for Sergeant Thomas because it was obvious he had some psychological problems that were not being treated. I asked the Warden if Sergeant Thomas was required to undergo any kind of counseling as a result of all this, and he said he actually mandated it as a condition of his continued employment because he knows Sergeant Thomas has some problems, and the only way he can maintain an authoritative position in the prison is to receive treatment until the counselor says he can stop. After hearing that news, I didn't worry about the situation anymore but instead focused on getting the class schedule together for the upcoming week.

We strolled on a little farther, admiring the natural beauty of the campsite while discussing the trifles of everyday prison life, and it finally occurred to me we could at least start the classes in the dining pavilion on the southern side of the camp since the work on that side was delayed until the scientists finished their research. The inmates residing in that area had already been equally divided and routed to the other three dining pavilions, so the classes would be completely undisturbed. The Warden thought it was a good idea and decided to wait until the scientists rendered their verdict before we started looking for another location. Now all I had to do was set up the time slots for each class we were going to hold this semester. But that was going to be easy because most of the inmates who registered had dropped their classes after we found out we were going to be working on Project IRZ. They didn't think we would still have class this semester. As a result, we only had a handful of students who were adamant about keeping pace with their anticipated graduation date. But the overall size of the classes didn't matter. What mattered was we were able to temporarily answer the location question that stumped us for a little while.

The Warden and I walked back to the main control unit to get an update on what the scientists were able to uncover so far. It was already after one o'clock, so we decided to discuss their progress over lunch. The Warden wasn't really comfortable having the scientists exposed to all the inmates yet since the scientists hadn't been formally told not to speak to the inmates. He decided to use our lunchtime today as an opportunity to educate them about the procedures at the campsite, especially those when they had direct contact with inmates. Subsequently, we had lunch away from the campsite at a restaurant in a town nearby. The Warden felt the gesture would be a nice icebreaker that would soften what he had to say later about the rules. The scientists didn't seem to mind because it gave them a chance to sightsee and have a big juicy T-bone steak the restaurant was famous for serving.

We all boarded the van and were chatting away about the clearing and some of the things the scientists had already uncovered. Dr. Cornell was the geologist in the group. He said he had been studying the rocks and stones they collected from the area and was able to determine with certainty that some of the smaller rocks were actually used for sharpening, which is why they were so oddly shaped. The blades of the stones they were used to sharpen had filed them down. He could also tell by the striations that they were old enough to be dated back about 700 to 800 years. He didn't have the equipment in the outdoor lab to distinguish their metallic properties, so he was going to ship a few of his samples to his research assistant in the lab at his university. When they finished examining the rocks, he said he would present the Warden with a full report of his findings. The Warden was pleased with Dr. Cornell's information and asked the other scientists how they were faring.

Dr. Brown is actually a renowned pedologist whose work has set many of the standards in modern science today. He said he was able to detect traces of substances found in the soil and knew definitely that one of those substances was blood. He, too, planned to ship some of his soil samples back to the lab at his university and also to a personal friend who was a hematologist. He wanted his friend to test the soil so she could tell us whether the blood belonged to humans, animals, or both. I was personally glad to hear it because we could use all the help we could get. So far, we had just enough evidence to support our original hypothesis that humans and possibly animals were killed at the clearing. Dr. Vinson and I weren't surprised by the scientists' news. We expected them to confirm that much of our preliminary findings. What we still didn't know was which ancient culture sacrificed humans in that area and if it safe for us to be there now. Of course, it would take longer for Dr. Vinson and the other anthropologists to make that determination. They had only begun their work today and the information they had was hardly enough for them to draw a conclusion. However, Dr. Harvard and Dr.Yale did say something peculiar that set off a train of thoughts in the Warden, Dr. Vinson, and me.

There were actually four anthropologists, including Dr. Vinson, in the group of scientists, but Dr. Harvard and Dr. Yale also had expertise in the reconstruction of ancient artifacts, including human bones. As expected, they concentrated their efforts on piecing together the bones and bone fragments they collected from the clearing to see if they actually had at least one complete human body to study. When the Warden asked them about the progress they were making, they said they were successful in rebuilding only parts of the bodies because they didn't have a full set of human bones yet. With all the bones and bone fragments they gathered from the clearing, we found it hard to believe they didn't have enough to rebuild at least one whole body. It just didn't seem possible, but they insisted they needed to go back to the clearing once more to make another collection. Dr. Vinson and I agreed to take them when we got back to the campsite, but Dr. Vinson was disturbed they couldn't reconstruct a body. He just knew they had enough bones and fragments because he was there when they collected them.

Distressed by their initial response, Dr. Vinson asked them what bones in particular were missing. The doctors replied they had just about all the bones except the ribs and the spine. I was sitting in the front seat and the Warden was driving the van. I turned completely around in slight disbelief and asked the doctor to repeat what he had just said. Dr. Yale obliged me and said a second time that the ribs and spine were missing from all the bones they collected. Dr. Vinson was sitting on the front row van seat with the two doctors. He took his glasses off and looked at both of them intently, asking them if they were trying to insinuate that the tribe who did this may have also believed in cannibalism. Dr. Vinson didn't really believe they were making an inference about cannibalism. It was simply a ploy to get them to say exactly what we were now suspecting. Unaware of Dr. Vinson's scheme, Dr. Harvard seemed a little offended with Dr. Vinson's question and responded rather frankly that he and Dr. Yale were not suggesting the former inhabitants were cannibals. If they wanted to say the people were cannibals, they would just say the people were cannibals. What he and Dr. Yale were trying to say was that all the bones normally found in a human torso were missing, and they could not construct a whole human body without them.

The Warden, now nervous and uncomfortable, caught Dr. Vinson's eyes in the rearview mirror when Dr. Yale finished speaking and told him to take the scientists back to the clearing with three more bags and to collect only bones this time. The Warden wanted to eliminate the possibility that we were dealing with the legendary murders Dr. Vinson told us about when he was first hired. He also decided to conceal the information about the dead politicians from the scientists. He wanted them to exhaust all their scientific possibilities before he disclosed or allowed Dr. Vinson to disclose anything to them about the murdered politicians with missing torsos. The Warden wasn't trying to deceive the scientists, but with all the effort he put into keeping certain information discreet, it didn't occur to the Warden that the scientists might have already known about the legend. After all, they were scientists who had spent years studying ancient culture. But since he wasn't comfortable telling them what he knew, he gave up his right to ask them what they knew. I turned around in my seat with my arms folded, staring out the window, and we all remained silent until we reached the restaurant.

The small rustic town was beautiful and quaint with wall-to-wall shops lined up on the main street. They even had a playhouse and small theater in the town square. There were well-manicured floral arrangements circling a lovely fountain in the town park that was situated in the center of town surrounded by the city hall, police and sheriff's office, post office, the town bank, an old museum, the steak house, and a pastry shop that featured homemade custards, cakes, donuts, and more sweet goodies. The smell of southern home-style cooking made my mouth water, and I felt like I was starving. I had eaten so much prison food I had nearly forgotten what homemade southern cooking tasted like. I was always at work or in a hurry, which left me little time to cook for myself, even though I was a pretty good cook. Naturally, the visits my mother made to my house were always considered precious because she could cook like no other.

We entered the restaurant and were immediately seated by a slender middle-aged waitress with long brown hair and a heavy southern drawl. She brought over eight glasses of water, a basket of buttermilk cornbread and sweet rolls fresh out of the oven, and a bowl of honey butter. The scientists weren't used to this kind of eating, so they dug into the cornbread and sweet rolls right away. By the time the waitress came back to take our orders, the breadbasket was empty. She smiled at the men, asking them if they liked the bread. Intrigued by their accents when they replied, she asked them where they were from, and they were all pleased to engage her because they enjoyed hearing her southern twang when she talked, too.

We made small talk over the cornbread, sweet rolls, and lemon-flavored iced tea the waitress brought while we waited for our orders. The Warden seemed to be in good spirits. That was a good sign because he usually looked worried or frustrated whenever we saw him, even when nothing was particularly wrong. Frowning had just become a natural aspect of his lifestyle that he was not going to change. Occasionally, he laughed and cracked jokes that were really funny, but most of the time he was a serious man who realized he was responsible for several lives. The scientists didn't seem to be bothered by his reserved facial expressions. They were actually enjoying themselves being in the south not strenuously working but still doing something they loved. Like Dr. Vinson, many of them carried around pictures of their grandchildren and told tales of fishing trips, science projects, music recitals, and a host of other grandparent delights. They were a pleasant group of men that I felt privileged to accompany.

After a hearty lunch, dessert, and an hour of stimulating conversation about our professional experiences inside and outside the prison, we headed back to the campsite to make another collection round at the clearing and wrap up today's business. The Warden told the scientists he wanted them to see if they could construct an entire human body by tonight, if they had the bones to do it. They assured the Warden the process was going to be quick because they already had all the other bones they needed; they just had to find some ribs and parts of the spine to determine the possible age and gender of the remains. The Warden wasn't really convinced he could rule out Dr. Vinson's legend, but it was worth a try to him.

As soon as we pulled up to the campsite, I jumped out of the passenger seat in the front and opened the side door of the van to let the scientists out. Dr. Vinson grabbed my hand, looking over the top of his glasses, and said the Warden was in denial. I nearly burst out laughing because although Dr. Vinson was being serious, it was funny how he said it and the way he looked at me when he spoke. The Warden pretended he didn't hear us and kept walking, but the other scientists asked Dr. Vinson what all the giggling was about. He shook his head and told them it was an inside joke and we kept walking. I tried to keep a straight face as we went back to the camp lab and prepared to leave for the clearing, but Dr. Vinson kept saying over and over that the Warden was in denial about the bones. It was funny, but he was right. It was becoming more apparent that the legend might have been true. The only proof we needed now was for the scientists to not find any ribs or parts of the spine again in this collection. That would sum up everything and the Warden wouldn't be able to deny it then.

We packed lightly, taking only what we needed for the collection, but this time I took a flashlight in case the scientists decided to stay much longer since they had more bags to fill.

Dr. Vinson gladly led the way through the woods beyond the slope stakes and past the small pond with the fish and the tadpoles. Instead of walking around the clearing as we had before, we simply walked right through it. There was no point in holding it completely sacred now because we had exhumed most of whatever was left and were returning for what we didn't get the first time. If our intent was to avoid disturbing whatever spirits were in that place, we should never have come there. But we had come, and now we had to find out whom the people were who lived there centuries before we arrived with our dozers and dump trucks.

The scientists were anxious to get back to the lab with this collection so they could try to assemble a body. If they were going to do it, this was their best chance. They didn't waste any time making this collection, and they only collected bones, except for the water sample they took from the small pond with the fish and the tadpoles on our way back to the camp. They rushed into the lab, emptied the contents of their knapsacks on the table, and worked nonstop in teams, assembling all the bones until they were completely finished. I sat there and watched them put each skull, arm, wrist, hand, and leg together, but none of them had a rib or a spine segment. We had collected five bags of bones total, and they were all missing ribs and spinal columns. The scientists were puzzled.

Dr. Vinson stood there looking somewhat amazed and somewhat relieved because he had some certainty about what happened in that area, but trepidation also came with that certainty because we were about to arouse a spiritual world we knew little to nothing about. All the scientists, except Dr. Vinson, sat down around the worktables trying to craft a reasonable explanation to describe how it could be possible for an expedition team to dig up human remains and not find one rib or spinal column in the entire area. The truth was that there was no reasonable explanation for it, and it was time for the Warden to tell these gentlemen about the dead politicians so they could stop trying to use science to explain something that wasn't scientifically possible.

I went next door to the main control unit and got the Warden, but he also brought Mr. Townsend with him. We entered the lab and Dr. Vinson and I took a seat away from the tables against the wall so the Warden could face the scientists without interference from either one of us. He saw the remains assembled on all the tables and asked the scientists what their results were, and they all told him they could only reconstruct what they had on the tables. He folded his arms with a hardened frown on his face that was more from confusion than anger and asked them to explain their position. Dr. Harvard and Dr. Yale told the Warden again, as they had before in the van, that there were no ribs and no spinal columns collected on either visit to the clearing, and they had no reasonable way to explain it. The Warden looked at Dr. Vinson with an expression that was curious to know if he had told his colleagues about the politicians. He didn't verbally ask, but Dr. Vinson just blurted out, "No," anyway. Mr. Townsend asked the Warden what the big deal was about the missing ribs and spinal columns. The Warden stood there staring into space, lost for words.

Mr. Townsend asked the Warden repeatedly if he was okay. The Warden finally broke his silence and stormed out of the tent. Dr. Vinson and I ran after the Warden to urge him to tell the scientists what he knew about the politicians so they could help us. He didn't want to break his code of silence because he didn't want Mr. Townsend to give the governor a negative report. He didn't have an issue with the scientists being told because Mr. Townsend had already sworn them to secrecy when they arrived. On the other hand, he had absolutely no control over what Mr. Townsend did or said and that troubled him. Just then, Mr. Townsend approached us outside the tent and demanded the Warden to tell him what was going on in that lab. The Warden refused, so Mr. Townsend threatened to call the governor and tell him the Warden was being insubordinate. The Warden still refused to talk, so Dr. Vinson told Mr. Townsend he would tell him everything because it wasn't worth the Warden losing his job.

We went back into the lab and waited for the Warden to bring some of the pictures of the mutilated politicians in so he could explain to Mr. Townsend and the scientists why the human remains on the tables in that lab were so important. He gave them enough information about the murders and the legend Dr. Vinson told us about for them to understand why we had to take every precaution necessary. He didn't tell them we had FBI agents working undercover in the general prison population, but he did tell them we were working indirectly with the FBI because Los Serpientes was known to use that ritual killing style, and the leader was currently housed in our prison. The scientists agreed to use their global resources to help us track down the killers, but Mr. Townsend was completely aloof and told the Warden he needed to move forward with the project and not heed a bunch of savage superstitions.

Dr. Vinson and the scientists pressed the Warden, reminding him rather bluntly that at the very least, he had an ethical responsibility not to desecrate a sacred burial ground. It didn't matter that the previous inhabitants weren't monotheistic. What mattered was we were now aware we were treading on ground consecrated for ritual killing, and we needed to make some effort to respect that. They told the Warden he needed to tell the governor himself about the bones and also remind the governor about the politicians. Perhaps the governor would be willing to suspend construction on that side of the camp a little longer until they fully understood the repercussions of awaking those ancient spirits. Mr. Townsend was absolutely livid and threatened to have the Warden fired if he didn't start construction on the south side of the camp as ordered. There was no way in hell he was going to allow the Warden to postpone construction any further because of angry spirits, Mexican gang members, or ancient legends. The scientists were furious now at Mr. Townsend's ignorance and insensitivity, and a heated argument followed, which left the Warden between a rock and a hard place. Unfortunately, his hands were tied. He knew Mr. Townsend outranked him. He had no choice but to start the construction as soon as possible.

CHAPTER NINE

The Warden waited about two days before he allowed the inmate work crews to take over on the south side of the camp. He intentionally delayed the work, citing possible safety issues and equipment problems for the delay, but we all knew it was to spite Mr. Townsend. Mr. Townsend had become a nuisance to everyone, especially the Warden. He followed the Warden everywhere he went, even to the bathroom. Collectively, we had great contempt for the man because he was a low-class tattletale, but there was nothing we could do about him being at the camp. We mutually avoided him as much as possible to make the situation tolerable. Also, if we had any planned meetings or information we intended to disseminate, we made a point not to include him.

Oddly, the first tree was not actually pushed down on the south side of the camp until late Wednesday morning after ten o'clock. Mr. Townsend had been out on that side of the project site with flashlights and shovels since about dawn, digging for God only knows what. But as long as he was out in the woods, the Warden couldn't afford to have his heavy equipment operators clearing that area. The combined noise from the heavy equipment, chain saws, and idling dump trucks was so loud that unless the workers saw Mr. Townsend before they got to him, they could accidentally run him over or cut him and not know it. The Warden certainly didn't want the liability of having to explain to the governor how Mr. Townsend was injured or possibly killed, so he held the workers up until Mr. Townsend was in plain sight of them. Then, he sent some officers to accompany Mr. Townsend back to the main control unit and made sure he stayed there.

Bewildered, Mr. Townsend came back empty-handed. He never said what he was looking for or what was so important about it that he had to look for it during that time of the morning. Even if he had, he made himself an enemy to everyone who had influence in the camp, so nobody was going to stick their neck out to help him find whatever he was looking for anyway. Besides all of this, his behavior was becoming stranger by the day ever since the argument Monday evening. He looked a mess as if he hadn't slept in a few days. He hadn't shaved; his hair was disheveled, clothes were wrinkled, and his eyes were noticeably red. His presence alone was an irritant for most of the officers, but to see him like this made us wonder if he was an alcoholic or a drug user. He literally looked like he was coming apart day after day. Maybe he was going through some kind of withdrawal. That might actually explain some of his obnoxious behavior. Whatever it was, it was beginning to take its toll on Mr. Townsend.

Now the officers manning the control unit didn't want Mr. Townsend hanging around them because it made them feel he was spying. They called Dr. Vinson on the radio and asked him to occupy some of Mr. Townsend's time. Dr. Vinson and two of his colleagues — Dr. Cornell and Dr. Brown — came to the main control unit and offered Mr. Townsend a slice of cake and a cup of coffee. All four of the men left the main control unit and took a light stroll toward the security tents where there was the least amount of noise. As one might expect, Dr. Vinson asked Mr. Townsend at length about his background and the kind of work he does for the governor. He asked Mr. Townsend about his family, his childhood, and other things people usually don't have reservations talking about. Mr. Townsend took the fact that these men were asking him questions as a sign of intellectual acceptance, but in reality they didn't accept him at all. Dr. Vinson and his colleagues were building a psychological profile of him, so we could know whom we were really dealing with.

They wandered on a little farther until they reached the northeastern perimeter of the camp where the security detail had a small pavilion all to themselves. The men sat down and talked for a while about politics, world events, and their current wish list of vacation spots. Dr. Vinson allowed Mr. Townsend to ramble on as much as he wanted to, feeling assured that if Mr. Townsend made himself comfortable enough, he might inadvertently let the cat out of the bag about what he was looking for. Mr. Townsend seemed troubled during the conversation, but Dr. Vinson pretended not to notice and began talking about fishing trips and science projects with his grandson, which opened the door for his colleagues to display pictures of their grandchildren, too. They all noticed something was obviously wrong with Mr. Townsend, but they didn't think it was the right time to ask him why he was out in the woods this morning. They let the matter rest and kept talking about their grandchildren. When Mr. Townsend completely withdrew himself from the conversation, they then decided to ask him what was wrong.

Dr. Vinson gave Mr. Townsend a general "Don't be afraid to ask for help" speech to ease into the conversation they really wanted to have with him. By this time, he was disconnected and apprehensive, but nobody knew why. Dr. Vinson and his colleagues were almost convinced now that perhaps he did have an addiction to something. Mr. Townsend insisted they were off base with their comments. He said that he was a social drinker but not an alcoholic, and he didn't use drugs at all. He didn't even smoke. Confused by his behavior, Dr. Vinson asked Mr. Townsend what was bothering him. Mr. Townsend denied having a problem, so Dr. Vinson asked him if everything was all right at home. Irritated by the redundant questions, Mr. Townsend began shouting at the men to mind their own business and he left them sitting at the table by themselves. Dr. Brown and Dr. Cornell asked Dr. Vinson if he wanted to take a casual stroll out into the woods later to see what Mr. Townsend was digging up. The trio agreed to do so and to bring their other colleagues with them.

They took their time going back to the main control unit, comparing their individual observations of Mr. Townsend as they went. Dr. Brown thought Mr. Townsend could have been a schizophrenic who wasn't taking his meds because his disposition went from one extreme to the other. When the scientists first met him a few days ago, he appeared to be a well-dressed but overbearing prick from the governor's office who was determined to make their lives as miserable as possible. Now he was a reclusive, unkempt mute walking aimlessly around the camp and in the woods at odd times during the wee hours of the morning. Nobody could explain his drastic change because he wasn't interactive with other people. He had been following the Warden around like a puppy, but that was only after he would come back from the woods and even then he never said much. They all had to admit his behavioral changes were unusual, but they couldn't put their finger on the immediate cause yet. They decided to discuss the matter further with the Warden when they got back to the main control unit.

The trio came back to their lab and waited for the work to come to an official end for the day. They knew the Warden would be preoccupied walking the grounds around the entire camp as long as he had equipment moving. Not to mention, there were several contract workers, including architects and construction supervisors, roaming around all four corners of the camp overseeing the work. With all these visitors around, the Warden made every effort to maintain safety and as much control of this site as possible. But we all understood what was at risk here, and we were fully prepared to deal with the long days and short nights we were going to have until this project was finished. That being said, we also did our parts to make the Warden's job as stress-free as we could, which sometimes meant not telling him about things until they got so bad we had to tell him because we needed his seal of approval to act on a resolution. But the Mr. Townsend business was a little different because he worked for the governor. We had to find a way to resolve this situation before it escalated into something much bigger.

It was almost seven o'clock in the evening, and we could still hear the heavy equipment in operation on the south side of the camp. The inmates had a longer workday today than normal because Mr. Townsend held them up this morning. Usually, work began at seven o'clock in the morning and ended at six o'clock in the evening. All the workers had a one-hour lunch from 11 AM to noon. It was scheduled that way to keep everybody on the same shift and because the Warden didn't want to risk having any avoidable accidents occur during dawn or dusk when there was too little light out to be operating heavy equipment or chain saws. There were enough facilities all over the camp to accommodate everybody at all times, so nobody had to stand in line for more than five or ten minutes to get anything. In fact, the inmates seemed to like this outdoor environment better than the caged facility they normally occupied, even though they slept on cots in twelve-man tents.

I entered the lab after I finished my own work for the day, and Dr. Vinson and the other scientists were already there waiting for the Warden. I knew Dr. Vinson and two of his colleagues had to babysit Mr. Townsend for a little while, so I asked them how it went. They all said the man was hiding something. I agreed and told them all I felt like maybe he was hiding something in the woods because he only went early in the morning when it was still dark and he was always alone. Since Dr. Cornell and Dr. Brown were babysitting with Dr. Vinson earlier this afternoon, Dr. Brown reiterated his idea that Mr. Townsend was possibly a schizophrenic who wasn't taking his medication. His behavior certainly supported the idea, but none of us really knew what was wrong with the man. We were all grasping at straws trying to figure him out. Finally, Dr. Vinson suggested we talk the Warden into having one of the physicians at the camp check the man out and give him a drug test. It sounded reasonable to the rest of us, so we mutually agreed to start there.

We could finally hear the Warden's voice outside the lab as he headed for the main control unit with a few of the construction supervisors. They were a little miffed because Mr. Townsend's hide-and-go-seek stunt threw them off schedule today. They were already two days behind to begin with, but with him parading around in the woods early in the morning, they were either going to have to work on their scheduled days off or work longer hours for a couple of weeks to get caught up. Being a durable man who operated well under pressure, the Warden told the supervisors not to worry about Mr. Townsend anymore. He said that he would make sure he didn't hinder their work further. They didn't seem all that convinced because the Warden wasn't loud and showed no emotion when he spoke, but they could rest assured he meant exactly what he said. The Warden hated embarrassment and was not about to have the governor send another snoop to his project site to figure out why his workers were further behind.

When we were sure the Warden was alone in the main control unit, we left the lab and went next door to see how he was faring and to get some insight on the overall progress of the project today. The Warden seemed optimistic and said all was well, but we had to do something about Mr. Townsend because he was interfering with the work and the construction supervisors weren't happy about it. The Warden asked Dr.

Vinson what happened when he came and got Mr. Townsend from the main control unit earlier. Dr. Vinson said they were talking and everything had seemed fine until he suddenly changed. Without warning, Mr. Townsend just shut down and left them out on the perimeter of the camp by themselves. The Warden asked the scientists what their professional opinion of Mr. Townsend was and Dr. Brown spoke up, suggesting Mr. Townsend undergo a preliminary physical to see if he had a substance abuse or drinking problem. The Warden thought it was a good idea, not just because Mr. Townsend really did act as if he was on drugs or something, but also because it gave him some leverage against Mr. Townsend. Dr. Brown said if an addiction problem could be ruled out, then they could start looking at possible mental illnesses he might be suffering from and get him help. The Warden said he would talk to Mr. Townsend about it privately first and have an officer assigned to accompany him wherever he went to see what he was up to. We left it at that and went to dinner.

Since the main control unit was in the center of the camp, we generally rotated which dining facility we were going to eat at on a daily basis because we were surrounded by all four of them. This evening, we decided to have dinner at the dining pavilion on the north side of the camp. All four sides had the exact same amenities and they all served the same food, so there was never a discrepancy about favoritism or partiality. By the time we got there, the dining facility had already been opened for over an hour. Most of the inmates and contract workers had already eaten and were on their way to the showers, laundry, commissary, or leisure areas to watch movies or work out. It was safe to say we had the place to ourselves except for a few latecomers who like to shop, shower, or work out first and then eat.

We always had a pretty good variety of food and the cooks weren't all that bad. Today's menu featured spaghetti with meatballs and sauce, fresh garden salad, and mixed veggies in the hot food line. If you preferred something from the fast food line, you could always have pizza, burgers, hotdogs, or burritos, served with fries, chips, potato salad, or coleslaw. For dessert, you could choose between two different kinds of cake, two different kinds of pie, cookies, and chocolate or vanilla ice cream. They also served sugar-free jello for the diabetics. The beverages included milk, soda, tea, water, and coffee. These were standard provisions supplied by the state and taxpayers, and we didn't take them for granted. There were several smaller states that couldn't afford to supply as much variety and as many condiments as we have. The inmates didn't complain either. Some of them were eating better meals in prison than they could ever get in the free world. Unfortunately, food was an incentive for them to come back.

Today had been a long day, and we were all glad it was coming to a close. The Warden said he was going to prep one of the doctors he trusted the most to deal with Mr. Townsend early in the morning before he had a chance to go to the bathroom. He also said he was going to call Sergeant Thomas and ask him who he would pick to shadow Mr. Townsend. Sergeant Thomas may have been temporarily suspended, but the Warden still called him whenever he needed information. We sat there in no hurry to leave the table, staring at nothing under the dining pavilion lights, talking about this and that, when Chaplain Beasley happened to see us sitting at the table. He said he had some interesting information he needed to share with us about a certain FBI agent we were working with.

Now the Warden didn't want him to say anything else at the moment because he hadn't told the scientists that we had undercover FBI agents working in the general population yet. The scientists had already seen them on several occasions because the agents were on a separate work detail and were always around, but they didn't know they were undercover. The Warden didn't want the scientists to know until he had an opportunity to check their individual backgrounds first. Since they all came back clean, he intended to call a surprise meeting at nine o'clock in the morning to formally introduce everybody except Mr. Townsend.

The Warden and Chaplain Beasley walked far enough from the table to not be heard. When the short conversation was finished, the chaplain left, and the Warden returned to join us at the table. I asked the Warden if everything was all right, and he said it was just as he suspected. The first thing that came to my mind was the double agent issue. The Warden finally knew who the mole was, or at least I thought he did. The Warden wouldn't tell us directly what Chaplain Beasley told him, but he said he had enough information now to start knocking down the house of cards Los Serpientes had been trying to build in our prison. Dr. Vinson asked the Warden if he knew who the dirty guards were. The Warden didn't know who all was accepting bribes, but he now knew who one of the major outside players was, and this information was colossal. Incidentally, he decided to tell us about the surprise meeting tomorrow. There was no point in keeping it a secret anymore since half the attendees were with him now. Afterward, he thanked us for our continued support, called it a night, and left us at the table, looking around at each other wondering what was going to be revealed.

After the Warden left, Dr. Vinson and I filled the other scientists in on some of the unclassified things that had been happening before they came on the scene. We felt it was only fair to them because they were now indirectly involved. They were using their global contacts to help us solve an issue that had nothing to do with them, and if they were willing to take this kind of risk, the least we could do was to make sure they knew as much as they needed to know about what they were getting themselves mixed up in. The Warden had already shown them the pictures of the politicians and made them aware of what Los Serpientes was, so they asked me and Dr. Vinson if we had personally met Cobra. We told them we had and would make sure they saw him face to face also. They didn't have to say anything to him, but they needed to know who he was now because their contacts were going to be receiving information about him and or people connected to him.

The scientists weren't the least bit angry; they were actually thrilled about being involved in all of this. Until their next expedition, this was all the excitement they were going to have. They spent most of their days glued to their campuses teaching classes. They love what they do and wouldn't trade it for anything, but this was enough to intrigue anybody who ordinarily didn't deal with this kind of stuff. They were glad to be on board and anxious to see the man we call Cobra. We didn't tell them how he looked with all the tattoos and such. We didn't want to give them our biased opinions of the man. We wanted them to judge him for themselves, and they would get that opportunity sometime this week after the Warden had the chance to filter the new information he wanted to share about the FBI agents.

Meanwhile, we, too, decided to end our discussion and head for our tents. I personally had a few loose ends to tie up with class schedules before I could go to bed, and the scientists had to go back to their lab so they box up some more samples they planned to ship out for research. We were all exhausted after a long day in and out of the woods in all four corners of this project site. Dr. Vinson landed himself a babysitting job while the Warden was scheming to force Mr. Townsend into taking a drug test. We never did go out into the woods to find out what Mr. Townsend was looking for. With all the other things going on around here, we didn't get to it today, but I knew we would tomorrow. In fact, when the Warden found out about it, he'll probably insist we go as soon as it is light before the workers begin clearing the rest of the area. Mr. Townsend won't know we went out there because he'll be with the doctor. That being said, I better lie down quickly. Daylight will be here in just a few hours.

My alarm went off at six o'clock as it normally does, but it was so hard for me to get up this morning. I don't know if it's the cot I'm sleeping on or the fact that I'm outside. This cot is very small, and sometimes I wake up stiff and groggy like I haven't slept enough or haven't slept at all. I haven't blown up my airbed yet because another professor is supposed to show up next week, or so they say. If she doesn't show, the mattress is coming out of the box for sure. Dr. Vinson came over and sat down on the empty cot in my tent. He asked me how I slept, but he was being sarcastic. He knew I didn't sleep well by the twisted, wrinkled pajamas I was wearing and the dried saliva trail running across the left side of my face. Nevertheless, I had to get going because we had to go hiking in the woods, and we had a nine o'clock meeting. I didn't know which one we were going to do first, but I suppose it didn't matter because they both had to be done.

As Dr. Vinson was leaving, I told him I would meet him in the dining pavilion on the eastern side of the camp for breakfast this morning. It was actually closer to the tent I slept in. . He agreed to meet me with his colleagues but said he was going to see the Warden first. I figured he was probably going to tell the Warden we were going to the woods to find what Mr. Townsend was looking for. He didn't actually say that, but I was pretty sure that that was going to be the bulk of his conversation this morning, along with getting the results back from Mr. Townsend's drug test. The Warden had one of the physicians administer a drug test on Mr. Townsend early this morning while it was still dark. I know Mr. Townsend would have been shocked when the officers came to get him, but he didn't have a choice. As long as he was at the campsite, the Warden had the authority to have everybody randomly tested for drugs, including Mr. Townsend.

I slow poked around a few minutes before dressing and finally leaving my tent. I wasn't really in a hurry this morning because I didn't have a lot to do today. I didn't really want to leave, but for the sake of keeping a regular schedule, I went to the dining pavilion to meet Dr. Vinson, but he wasn't there yet. I went through the line and ordered whatever I felt up to eating and grabbed a cup of coffee on my way to an unoccupied table. I assumed Dr. Vinson was probably still with the Warden and that his colleagues were waiting for him in the lab next door to the main control unit. They usually did everything together like men in a fraternity. I sat down and began eating my whole grain waffle topped with diced fruit and a bowl of hot oatmeal with a spoonful of butter and brown sugar. Other than the usual buzz from the sound of multiple conversations between inmates in the dining pavilion, it was pretty quiet. Today was Thursday and we were all ready for Friday to come and go so we could enjoy our first weekend off.

I had finished eating and realized I had waited for Dr. Vinson for almost an hour. It wasn't like him to not show up or not call if he couldn't make it. I didn't hear any traffic on the radio this morning, and I know he wouldn't have gone into the woods without telling me first, especially since we were supposed to go together. I figured he probably got caught up in a deep conversation with the Warden. Therefore, I left the dining pavilion and decided to finish my work early so I could sneak a nap in sometime this afternoon. I had a few things I needed to do, which required going to the main control unit anyway. I could easily check in with everybody while I was there.

I grabbed my knapsack and started walking to the control unit to use the computer so I could finish my work. I had a laptop back in my tent, but working alone today would've made me sleepier than I already was, and I really wanted to wait until after lunch to lie down. Everything was quiet as I got closer to the control unit. In fact, it was too quiet, and that began to disturb me. Normally, there would people walking around the camp all day until it was time to go to bed. Even then, there were people randomly walking back and forth to the bathrooms. I could hear some of the heavy equipment being cranked at a distance. Still, there were too few inmates and contract workers out for this to be a normal workday. There should've been thousands of people walking around this camp. Instead, there were only hundreds. Something was wrong with this picture. I needed to find out what it was.

I entered the control unit, and there sat the Warden, the scientists, and Mr. Townsend, looking somber and confused. As soon as I walked in, the Warden asked me to join him and the others at the table in the center of the tent. My right arm was still looped in one of the straps on the back of my knapsack. I sat the bag down on the table in front me, pulled out a chair, and slowly sat down, watching the men's facial expressions as I sat. The Warden was sitting at the left end of the long rectangular table with his hands folded and his usual half frustrated, half anguished look on his face. I looked around the table at the faces of these men to see if I could make eye contact with one of them since no one was talking yet. They were all looking down at the table or the ground or something in that vicinity. I cleared my throat to break the dead silence. Still, no one spoke. Finally, I asked the Warden what he needed to tell me because I knew by now that it was something very important and possibly personal.

He sighed and hesitated for a moment and then said that we had a problem. I asked him to elaborate on the problem. The Warden said I wasn't going to believe it, but Mr. Townsend didn't have a substance abuse problem and there was no alcohol in his system. I didn't respond right away because I felt that there was something more serious about to follow the Warden's comment. He took my silence as a cue to continue on and said that the reason why Mr. Townsend had been in the woods was because he was trying to return the bones we dug up from the mounds. He had been hearing the voices of children screaming in the woods and figured that we had disturbed the dead children's spirits when we took the bones for research. The Warden said Mr. Townsend now believes we angered the gods that received these children as sacrifices, and these gods were going to wreak havoc on us for desecrating their sacrificial mounds, so we needed to stop the project on the south side of the camp.

I remained silent but was furious at the news because this was the same coldblooded, arrogant person who threatened to have the Warden fired less than a week ago when we initially suggested that construction on the south side of the camp be delayed further until we found out more about the mounds and the people who inhabited this region. Now that he hears things at night and can't sleep, we should officially stop construction. I gazed at Mr. Townsend for several minutes with the burning desire to reach out and punch him in the face. If I could stare daggers in that man, he would've been repeatedly stabbed to death. However, I managed to compose myself and took a deep breath and asked Mr. Townsend how he intended to explain all of this to the governor. As slovenly as he looked, he still had the audacity to say he wasn't going to explain anything to the governor. He was going to use the scientists to do it.

There were no raised eyebrows, no vehement protests, and no emotional responses from Dr. Vinson or his colleagues. They just calmly said, "No." When the scientists refused, the old Mr. Townsend was resurrected long enough for him to threaten them the way he had the Warden, but they all burst out laughing. He became extremely angry, and his face and neck turned fire truck red. His lips were drawn in, and you could see veins sticking up on the surface of his forehead and neck. He pounded his fist on the table, swearing at the men for laughing at him, but they continued as if they hadn't heard him at all. Realizing he couldn't get the best of them, he folded his arms, sulking in his chair until Dr. Vinson stopped laughing long enough to speak plainly to him.

When Dr. Vinson finally did stop laughing, he became serious very quickly and reminded Mr. Townsend of his unwillingness to hear us when we suggested construction be delayed until we had adequate information about this area. Dr. Vinson also made it clear to Mr. Townsend that neither he nor his colleagues would be used to do his bidding, and whatever scientific information they had would remain undisclosed. If Mr. Townsend wanted the governor to know what was happening at the camp, he would have to tell the governor himself. Mr. Townsend then feigned concern and became seemingly apologetic, trying to persuade us to stop the project by saying we would all be morally responsible for anything that happened from now on if we didn't. The more he talked, the angrier I became. As far as I was concerned, he was in no position to tell us about moral responsibility. Notwithstanding, the damage had been already been done. The area was already being cleared, and there was no way the trees, shrub, grass, or dirt could be put back in place as it was before it was disturbed. It was gone.

I told Mr. Townsend he was a parasitic person who needed some serious psychiatric help if he believed putting the bones back in whatever was left of the mounds would stop the desecration. I told him it didn't work that way. Once you dug up something, it is dug up. Even if you put it back in the ground or wherever you found it, it has still been disturbed from its original place of rest. If he's afraid now that we are going to face some spiritual cataclysm as a result of this project, he'll just have to live with that on his conscience. I then told him I was not going to be morally responsible for anything; he was going to be responsible because it was his decision to push the project forward when we wanted to delay it.

Mr. Townsend started pounding his fist into the table again, shouting we didn't understand and that we needed to listen to him. It's not that we didn't understand. The problem was we actually did understand, but there was nothing that we could do about it now. We all felt as if we were going to set off something supernatural when we became aware of the clearing and the mounds. It was an unspoken eerie feeling we all privately shared. That's why we were eager to get the scientists in to conduct the research. We knew we were going to open a portal to something or somewhere that we didn't want to have opened if we cleared that area, but thanks to Mr. Townsend, it was too late now. The heavy equipment was already in the area, rolling over exposed skulls, smashing shallow graves, and pushing whatever was left of the mounds down. Whatever spirits we have awakened as a result of this, we would all have to face. The only thing we could do now is just pray as we go and wait for it to happen. But if Mr. Townsend feels as if he can fight against these spirits, then he can fight that battle alone. I have a hard enough time fighting the living; I can't even imagine what it would be like to fight the dead.

CHAPTER TEN

It was Friday evening and our first weekend was finally here. It had been an unbelievable week with the arrival of Mr. Townsend, the project delays, the scientific discoveries, and other unexpected things. I was so exhausted I strongly considered skipping dinner. I wanted to shower and go straight to my tent. I didn't want to hear music. I didn't want to read. I didn't want to watch a movie. I didn't want to do anything except sleep tonight. I had laundry to do over the weekend, and I needed to read over my lesson plan again no later than Sunday because my first outdoor class was this coming Monday. Of course, some of the inmates who were scheduled to take to my class had already stopped me during the week and told me they were looking forward to being in my class this semester. I suppose I was ready for class to begin, too. I had been out of my element with all this anthropology and spy business. I was glad to be getting back to what I love: teaching.

It was nearly seven o'clock, and Dr. Vinson had come by to see if I would be joining him and the others for dinner. I really enjoyed their company, but I was so tired I actually turned him down. He was a little disappointed but said he understood and would come back in about an hour or so with something for me to eat from the dining pavilion. He knew I had been having a difficult time sleeping on that cot, but that was about to change. It just so happens that the other professor never showed up, so this was also going to be the first night I slept on my airbed. I had been secretly counting the days, hoping she wouldn't show. I would have to add more time segments to my class load to accommodate her absence, but it was a trade I was happy to embrace.

When Dr. Vinson came by, I was actually in the process of setting up my mattress and preparing for a shower and bed shortly thereafter. I had put some papers out on my cot that I needed to look at before I went to sleep, but they were nothing major. My father had sent me a letter a couple of days ago, but I hadn't gotten around to reading it yet. I decided to read his letter and write him back tonight. If I waited too long to respond, it would concern him, and he would start making phone calls. I needed to write him anyway to tell him about the clearing and the mounds. He isn't an anthropologist, but he has friends in high places who know other people in high places who have access to information on everything. If the scientists couldn't find out about this area, my father could. In fact, I wouldn't be surprised at all if my father already knew about the mounds in general. He reads a lot and about every subject that exists. As well, he knows Dr. Vinson. They may have already communicated about the clearing and the mounds for all I know. I have always suspected that Dr. Vinson knew more than he let on, but keeping secrets isn't exactly a crime.

Before Dr. Vinson left my tent, we had a brief conversation about what Mr. Townsend told us yesterday. Dr. Vinson asked me if I honestly believed we were about to experience some unexplainable supernatural things, and I told him I thought we were. He told me he felt the same way and his colleagues did, too. He said he and the Warden had a pretty deep conversation last night about the infinite possibilities of what might happen, and the Warden decided to call in another truck to bring more safety equipment and medical supplies. The Warden said if we couldn't stop whatever was coming, the least we could do was try to respond to it and be prepared to deal with the aftermath. He said the trucks would be coming in sometime Saturday evening. I was a little anxious now because the Warden was a skeptic who didn't believe in anything, but if he called for backup then we needed to treat every situation as if it was critical.

I came back from the shower and finished the letter I was intending to send my father. Receiving his letters was always a pleasant surprise because they were funny. He would begin each letter with a formal heading and salutation, and the first paragraph would be about something church related. The next few paragraphs were always about current events: funerals, weddings, newborn babies, graduations, or somebody getting a job if he or she was not known to retain employment for long periods of time. He would then close the letter with something church related again and maybe a Bible verse. Often, he wrote about relatives I never knew because they were old when I was born or perhaps the last time I saw them was when I was three or four years old. He would always ask me if I remembered who they were, and I would always say, "No." Somehow, he never remembered that I said, "No," in the previous letter, and he would write me another letter asking me if I remembered this person or that person all over again. His letters were priceless. I wanted to make sure the letter to my father went out promptly with the next mail delivery, so I sealed and stamped the enveloped and set it on my desk for the postal run Saturday afternoon. I prayed, blew out the scented candles on my desk, and stretched out under my comforter on my airbed. I took one last look at my clock, and it was almost 8:15 PM. I closed my eyes, and before I knew anything, I was fast asleep.

The sound of thunder and torrential rain had awakened me during the middle of the night. A few drops of water had fallen on the floor of my tent near my bed. The ground underneath my tent was covered with a thick mat that had interlocking hooks fastened to the bottom of the tent. The tent had a hard surface, which made the drops of water falling from the roof of the tent sound like small rocks when they struck it. I lit the wick inside my kerosene lamp and sat up in my bed, waiting for my eyes to bring everything into focus in the dim light. The more conscious I became of the rain, the louder it sounded. I pushed my covers back yawning, half awake and hungry from missing dinner. I was pretty good at keeping up with the weather report, but I didn't remember anything in this week's report about rain in our area. As a matter of fact, it was supposed to be hot and dry for the next two weeks, according to the meteorologists I listen to, but it was a trivial issue I wasn't particularly curious about. Besides, the weather people can't always get it right, and I've never had a problem sleeping when it rained anyway.

I looked around the tent to make sure I didn't have any major water leaks and I happened to notice a plate of food on my desk that Dr. Vinson brought in for me as he promised. There was a jumbo-sized cheeseburger with the works, fries, two cans of orange soda, a cup of melting ice, two big peanut butter cookies, and a wordless note with a big smiley face. My hunger problems were solved and I didn't even have to leave my bed. When I finished wolfing down my food, I was definitely going back to sleep.

Life was going to be beautiful again for the time being. I had about ten hours of bliss to take advantage of, and I intended to milk those hours until the very last second. I ate as much as I had an appetite to eat while the rain kept pitter-pattering on my tent with an occasional drop here and there falling on the floor inside my tent. The sound of those isolated drops provided me with some rhythmic therapy. As each drop hit the floor, I felt a drop of anxiety about the clearing and the mounds leave me. No matter what happened, I believed I would have the fortitude to deal with it. But for now, I wanted to take my fortitude back to bed, so I put the plate with my burger fragments back on my desk, blew out the lamp, and went back to sleep, satisfied and full.

My alarm went off at six o'clock in the morning as it usually does. This morning, I actually felt rested and fresh. I didn't know how muddy the ground was going to be outside, but I had to see if I could make my way through it so I could get to the main road for my morning run. I stayed in bed gradually waking up until about 7:15 AM. I wasn't in a hurry to get up because I knew I couldn't go running until it was completely light outside. The Warden didn't allow anything to go on, including operating equipment or leaving the camp, at dawn or dusk. He was a stickler for security and those were the rules. There were some exceptions where security was involved, but as a general rule, if it could be done in the light, then it was.

I finally dragged myself up and got dressed, reluctant to leave my comfy bed. I needed to make my round in the bathroom first before I was ready to go running. It was completely light outside, and I could hear others stirring about now. The buzz from their conversations kept getting louder and louder, and more people were waking up and going outside. I looked at the clock and saw it was only 7:45 AM. Why were all these folks getting up so early on their first day off? Maybe the inmates had a meeting I didn't know about. Perhaps they were doing some kind of health and wellness sweep. We did have those from time to time just to make sure no one was injured or sick and not receiving treatment, but that couldn't have been the answer because I had to do part of the screening when we had a health and wellness sweep. Whatever the reason was, I'd find out soon enough when I finished lacing up my shoes and securing the rest of my hygiene supplies.

Dr. Vinson stormed into my tent, looking over the wire-rim glasses he had resting on the tip of his nose. I was startled by his abrupt entry but managed to blurt out a halfway decent sounding, "Good Morning." He stood there with his fingers interlocked in front of him and said, "You don't know do you?" I was sitting on my bed tying my shoes when he asked the question. I didn't know how serious he was until I looked up and saw his face. I asked him what was wrong and what was I supposed to know. He said that whatever we stirred up at the clearing was upon us now. I stopped tying my shoes altogether and sat up completely, pausing before I spoke. I looked in Dr. Vinson's eyes to see if there were signs of horror or regret or both. I asked Dr. Vinson if he was sure that whatever happened or was happening was tied to the clearing. He nodded and then said he was fairly certain we had released something demonic into the atmosphere. I asked him if he had infallible proof. He nodded again. I asked him to show me, and he opened the door of my tent so I could walk out first.

When I stepped out, I noticed the pools of water and fallen limbs and leaves left behind from the storm covering most of the ground in front of me. My tent faced the tree line, so I couldn't see much else. I didn't know what I was supposed to be looking for, so I started looking for anything that would stand out. Dr. Vinson told me to walk out a little further from my tent and look at the ground that wasn't covered with limbs and leaves, and I would see it then. I walked a few feet away from my tent and turned around to see the ground around my tent because there were no trees between the tents. That's when I saw it.

I wouldn't have believed it if I hadn't seen it with my own eyes. The ground was covered with dead birds. They were all on the ground between the tents where there were no trees for them to take shelter from the storm, which made their appearance all the more striking. Birds knew to take shelter when a storm was coming; it was part of their instinctive nature. But even if they didn't take shelter, rain was not considered lethal to them. If lightning was the cause then it might only strike one individual bird at a time, not a whole campsite full. If it was something deadly in the rain itself, dead birds would have been on the ground inside and outside the camp, but these birds had fallen dead only between our tents. Why weren't dead birds lying on the outside of the camp? What were the odds of something rare like this happening? Could it be logically explained? I didn't think so, and apparently Mr. Townsend didn't either because he started running through the camp screaming at the top of his lungs that we should all get out because demons were there.

By this time, just about everybody working on the project site was awake, outside, and bewildered. They were all asking questions about why the birds were on the ground. I didn't have a philosophical answer and neither did Dr. Vinson, but we couldn't have a loose cannon like Mr. Townsend hobnobbing throughout the camp, spreading fear with stories about the clearing and other things the inmates didn't need to know. We had to find a way to silence him; otherwise, we might have a mutiny on our hands. The Warden made a general call out on the radio for the officers to do the morning count early so he could muster the inmates in areas away from the dead birds. He knew that as long as they stood there gazing at the lifeless birds on the ground, a sense of panic would gradually overcome them one by one. It also gave us a chance to drag Mr. Townsend into a tent with one of the doctors so they could bind, gag, and inject him with a sedative that would keep him out of sight for at least twelve hours.

With tens of thousands of heads to count, the process usually took two to three hours, which gave the FBI agents assigned to do odd jobs a chance to rake the birds up in a pile and burn them. The scientists bagged up several birds to take to the lab, but the rest were destroyed. The Warden then called an emergency meeting with the committee members to make sure everybody knew what was going on and to see what our thoughts were about the situation. When the Warden told the chaplains and the FBI agents about the clearing and formally introduced the scientists to the rest of the committee members, they all willingly agreed to be receptive to whatever scientific information Dr. Vinson and his colleagues could present that might help us.

Consequently, the scientists began educating us about the former inhabitants of the area and about their ritual beliefs. They told the other committee members about the bones they collected and some of the results they got back from their university laboratories. Everyone in the tent remained silent, so the scientists continued on telling us about the tools these ancient people used, the foods they may have eaten, and other things, which brought us back to the legend Dr. Vinson originally told us about several months ago. When all the scientists finished speaking, the Warden opened the floor for discussion and gave everybody an equal chance to express his or her own opinion.

Without hesitation, Chaplain Beasley alluded that events like these usually brought temporary but immediate spiritual awareness for people who weren't generally religious, so he and the other chaplains were going to publicly but subtly spread the word that they were available for counseling, confession, Communion, and baptism for all who decided to get closer to God. The Warden thought it was a good idea for the chaplains to be seen more often throughout the camp, too. He felt it would be good for morale. Dr. Vinson and I believed the chaplains saw this as an opportunity to improve their reputations more than helping the inmates. The inmates didn't trust them at all because the chaplains always acted like double agents. Even if they did baptize inmates or perform Communion services, they were still phony as far as we were concerned, but I guess it wasn't that big of a deal because they couldn't be any more pretentious now than they had already been in the past.

The scientists said they would keep us up to date with every shred of information they got back from their universities. The Warden asked the FBI agents if they had anything to contribute to the conversation, and at first they looked a little puzzled and remained silent. Then one of the FBI agents, Ramón Ducati, hesitantly said he had worked on an undercover prison detail a few years ago and supposedly there was an inmate the Hispanics called El Chamán, or the Shaman, serving a double life sentence in solitary confinement at a Supermax prison somewhere in the state of Kansas. Chaplain Beasley immediately interrupted agent Ducati before he could finish and strongly objected to having any dealings whatsoever with this inmate. He said the man was completely deranged, extremely dangerous, and was heavily involved in a variety of witchcraft practices. The Warden asked Ducati if what Chaplain Beasley said was true. Agent Ducati said the inmate wasn't deranged — delusional maybe, but not deranged — and for decades he had practiced Hoodoo, Santeria, and other forms of witchcraft that often involved blood sacrifices, which is why they needed to contact El Chamán all the more. He was an expert on these things, and if nobody knew how to fight or stop this force controlling this area, the Shaman would. The Warden pulled out a chair to sit down at the left end of the rectangular table, questioning Ducati's scruples all the while. Everybody remained silent while the Warden ranted on about never having been in this kind of predicament in all his twenty-something years as a prison warden and about how he didn't need a craft worker trying work some black magic in an atmosphere that was already polluted with some kind of black magic. He said he wasn't interested in playing host to the battle of the dark powers.

Agent Ducati didn't want to aggravate the Warden any more than he felt necessary, but he pressed the Warden, mildly suggesting it might be worth a shot to talk to this inmate because he knew about all these rituals. After all, he practiced them. The reason why he was incarcerated in the first place was because he butchered several people for his beliefs in the craft. Skeptically, the Warden asked Ducati why none of this inmate's "craftwork" was ever reported. Agent Ducati said there were no reports because the bodies were never found. The Warden then asked the inevitable question, which was how anybody knew this guy was a murderer. Chaplain Beasley quickly jumped in to answer, saying even though they never found a body, they knew he was a killer because they watched the video tapes he made of the ritual killings.

Everyone in the room was now filled with skepticism and a little fear. But Agent Ducati insisted we remain objective about the issue. After all, we didn't have any leads. He told the Warden it wouldn't hurt to talk to the Shaman because it was better to have too much information than to not have any. Reluctantly, the Warden agreed with his point and said he would consider it but only after we exhausted whatever resources we had, which definitely meant somebody was going to see this man because we didn't have any resources, so that matter was somewhat resolved for now. We still had to figure out what we were going to do about Mr. Townsend because we couldn't afford to have any of this leaked to the public. We had to keep it contained as much as possible.

The Warden told all the officers who normally checked inmate mail to make sure the inmates didn't write home about any of the strange things that were beginning to happen. If they did, the officers were supposed to throw their letters in the trash. If the inmates asked or complained about their family members not receiving their mail, they were supposed to apologize and blame the local post office for the mix up. Next, the Warden set a plan in motion to control information being passed from the contract workers on our site. He said he was going to remind them that they had all signed affidavits to keep all information about the project to themselves, but if any of them leaked anything to the press about our site, the Warden said he was going to have the doctors cook up some medicinal cocktails and spike their food and beverages so they could fail a planned random drug test and be fined. If that didn't work, he was going to have them framed for some petty crimes and removed from the project altogether. Of course, the misdemeanor charges would later be dropped. These tactics were dirty and underhanded, but it was all we could do for the time being.

The last thing the Warden did was to ask all of us to vote on whether we wanted to involve the Shaman in this situation or not. Personally, I didn't care as long as I didn't have to go see the man. I wasn't afraid of going to the prison, but I hated visiting inmates in solitary confinement because it was the severest form of confinement there was in prison. Moreover, it takes a lot to get used to seeing humans living in cages, but to see them in even smaller cages without windows where they are kept twenty-three hours a day, eating, sleeping, and defecating, makes you bitter that we even have prisons in our society. Nevertheless, the Warden told us to use the secret passwords he gave us when we first arrived at the camp to cast our votes that way no would feel pressured about voting a certain way. Every committee member would cast a vote and the majority vote was final. He handed all twelve of us a slip of paper and he voted too so there could be no tie. When all the votes were in, he asked one of the scientists to read the votes while he kept score. The decision was made: we were going to see the Shaman.

After we voted, the Warden asked the scientists if they would team up with some of the doctors to do some lab work on the dead birds to see if there was anything toxic in their bodies at all. He told me he wanted me to pair up with Dr. Vinson to continue researching the area and to get some more in depth information about the legend of Los Antiguos. He figured if we had let them out of some dimension then there had to be a way for us to force them back in. The Warden then asked the FBI agents if they had any new information about Los Serpientes, but the agents planted inside the gang all said that Los Serpientes seemed to be on hiatus since we were working on the project. Whatever the Woods were doing, they were doing on the own because Los Serpientes weren't moving anything right now, at least not the group at our prison.

The Warden said it wasn't possible for the Woods to be pushing dope in the prison unless they were pushing it for Los Serpientes. They didn't have extensive drug connections like the other gangs did. Dr. Vinson asked the Warden if he had ever considered the fact that maybe Los Serpientes were being set up. Granted, they formed a vicious gang with a hand in everything criminal, but it just didn't make sense that they would risk getting caught selling their own drugs in prison for nickels and dimes when they make millions on the streets. Besides, anybody could easily commit a crime and blame Los Serpientes, and law enforcement would suspect them strictly because of their reputation. Agent Alvarez blurted out that Dr. Vinson needed to stick to science and let the FBI deal with the criminals.

Looking over the top of his glasses, Dr. Vinson asked Agent Alvarez why he was so defensive because it was quite possible we had been in looking in the wrong place all along. Agent Alvarez became angry and started raising his voice at Dr. Vinson, saying that criminals are sophisticated individuals who know when to lay low so they can temporarily detract attention from themselves. Dr. Vinson swiveled his body in his chair facing the agent and crossed his legs before he reiterated his point a bit more emphatically to the Warden and the other committee members that we could be wrong, and it would be reckless for us to not consider other suspects. Agent Alvarez started yelling at Dr. Vinson and right in the middle of it all, the Warden interjected and told Alvarez that if he didn't know any better, he would think that the matter was personal for him the way he was yelling and taking sides. Agent Alvarez turned blood red in the face and got up and stormed out of the tent. Some of the chaplains and other FBI agents were confused, looking around at each asking what that was all about. The Warden never said a word but he made eye contact with Chaplain Beasley, which signaled to Dr. Vinson and me that another big secret was about to unfold.

After Agent Alvarez stormed out of the tent, the Warden dismissed the other agents and released them back into the general population so they could be seen by the inmates during the morning head count. When they left the tent, the Warden told us that he and Chaplain Beasley had the undercover FBI agents checked out and one of them was dirty. The chaplain had previously mentioned in part that he had some damaging information on an FBI agent who may have been working with us but wasn't sure of it. He said he was going to contact an old friend that worked a case with him to get all the details. Chaplain Beasley said he had given his friend all the names of the agents working with us, and his friend was able to gain access to their personnel files. After his temper tantrum, it was no surprise to find out that Agent Alvarez was dirty. In fact, he wasn't demoted only because he leaked information that caused another officer to be killed; he was also disciplined for planting evidence at specific crime scenes that involved drugs.

The Warden continued on telling us that when the investigators came out to inventory the crime scenes Alvarez was working, the evidence would indicate a particular syndicate's trademark. Since there weren't usually any witnesses, or any witnesses willing to give a statement, the only information investigators had to go on was the planted evidence. For a season, the FBI thought maybe these criminal enterprises were leaving evidence and becoming sloppy because they felt like they couldn't be touched. They had enough money to hire the best criminal defense attorneys in the business. After a while, the FBI began to notice a pattern with the evidence, and it appeared that certain organizations, although criminal, were being unlawfully targeted. Internal Affairs decided to audit several cases and found evidence from old cases that were already logged reappearing at new crime scenes. They secretly placed several agents under surveillance and caught Alvarez who, to this day, claims he was framed. That being the case, it seems likely that he was assigned or willfully asked for this assignment so he could plant evidence against Los Serpientes.

Currently, that's a theory that can't be proven yet because Los Serpientes is not moving anything, but it's just a matter of time before Alvarez makes his move. However, he can't do it alone. He has to have another contact involved in this, especially since he has members of the Ecumenical Community using their contacts to bring the drugs in. Dr.

Vinson asked Chaplain Beasley if Alvarez had any contacts that were documented in his old case files that we needed to know about. The chaplain couldn't say for sure, but he did say he had an even bigger bomb to drop on us about Alvarez. He said that Alvarez and Cobra were related through marriage. They knew each other personally so it was possible they were working together in all of this. Alvarez had enough informants to keep him aware of whom he could trust on the streets, and Cobra had enough cartel members on his list of associates to traffic an endless supply of illegal drugs. The Warden interjected that there was also an alternate theory, which suggests Alvarez may be playing Cobra behind his back. Alvarez could be moving the drugs himself but making it look as if Cobra's gang was behind it all. After all, he does plant evidence at crime scenes when he wants to target a particular group.

Dr. Vinson asked the Warden if it was safe to assume now that Alvarez was the double agent, and the Warden said it was. I asked the Warden how he intended to find out who the other mice were since he had the big rat now. He said he still had his mole planted in the general population to feed him information. He said he was going to do some strategizing to come up with a foolproof plan to catch him. In the meantime, the Warden didn't want us to tell anybody that we knew about Alvarez. He didn't even want us to talk about it. He couldn't afford to take any risks with information now, which included all private visits to see the Shaman. The Warden officially nominated Dr. Vinson and me to go see the man.

About that time, one of the officers came into the main control unit to tell the Warden that all the birds were removed and the count was done. It was Saturday, the first day of the first weekend we had off work, so the Warden decided to have an impromptu cookout to ease the tension. The cooks were the only inmates on the project site who worked shorter shifts than all the other inmates. They worked eight-hour shifts around the clock, and since the cookout was spur-of-the-moment, the cooks who normally worked the afternoon shift were called to duty to help the morning shift cooks. The night shift cooks had just finished work around the time the ruckus was going on with the birds outside, so they went to bed along with most of the inmates and workers who were awakened. The officers had already spread the word throughout the ranks that there was going to be a cookout today, so many of the inmates went back to bed until lunch time. Meanwhile, the committee members and I got busy working on our assignments for a few hours before taking a break.

I finally got a chance to go for my run, but by the time I did, it was during the early part of the afternoon and you could smell the mesquite logs burning on the grills a mile away. Normally, I take all my frustrations and anger out on the road and leave them there when I'm running.

For me, running is not mere exercise; it is nonverbal therapy that helps me cope with everything and everybody around me. But this run was different. The weight of all my thoughts was just too heavy for me to release in one running session. I thought the raindrops were going to be enough but that was before I awoke to a campsite full of dead birds. This situation was becoming more precarious by the day. Unfortunately, we didn't even know what we were really fighting and going to see the Shaman was definitely not on my to-do list, but as the old saying goes, "Plans are made to be broken." Thus, the only planned event in my schedule now is school.

CHAPTER ELEVEN

The weekend had passed rather quickly and I was sick as a dog. I had a high fever, a sour stomach, and I was extremely nauseated. The mere smell of food made me sick. It was almost as if I had all been exposed to some form of food poisoning or water contamination. But I wasn't just sick. I could hardly remember anything that happened. For example, Saturday had come and gone, and the only thing I remembered accomplishing was going running sometime that afternoon and bagging up laundry to wash on Sunday that never got washed. I remembered walking outside early Saturday morning and there were dead birds everywhere around the tents, but there were no birds on the ground in the woods where all the trees were. I remembered sitting in a chair behind most of the inmates at one of the dining pavilions for Sunday service. I remembered the sound of one of the hymnbooks striking the ground when it was dropped during the service because I already had a headache before the book fell, so it irritated me. I remembered hearing Chaplain Beasley slam his hand down on the makeshift podium during his Sunday morning message. I even remembered the unusual benediction he gave as the service ended, but that's all I really remember from the entire weekend. I don't know if I showered, reviewed my lesson, or even ate.

Dr. Vinson came to see me, and judging from the brightness of the sunlight pouring into the windows of my tent, I assumed it was well past morning. I guess I had been feeling so weak and ill that I slept through the morning and into the early part of the afternoon. He knelt down beside my bed and placed a warm compress across my forehead, softly asking me how I was feeling. I was still groggy, but my thoughts and sense of awareness were beginning to come together. I began slowly raising myself up in bed so I could sit up and look around my tent to inventory what I may or may not have done. I asked him to tell me what had been happening over the weekend because the last thing I remembered was that stupid benediction Chaplain Beasley gave at the end of Sunday's service. Dr. Vinson reminded me the benediction sounded stupid because the chaplain tried to tell a joke nobody got the gist of. Bits and pieces of the joke came back to me then, and I remembered laughing after he told the joke because there was so much dead silence in the audience that you could hear a ball of cotton fall on the ground.

Dr. Vinson had brought me a bottle of 7-Up to settle my stomach and a bowl of hot soup that he encouraged me to eat if I felt up to it. He said the soup and soda were safe because they didn't come from the food supplies that were shipped into the camp. He had bought these items before he came here and packed them with the rest of the things he had planned to bring to the camp. I didn't have much of an appetite at the moment, but I knew I needed to eat something so I could gain some strength. I sat up and ate the bowl of soup and took a few swigs of soda, which did make me feel better. I thanked him for not just the food and beverage but also for his overall care and concern. After I finished the soup, I took an orange out of my cooler and began peeling it for us to share while he made me aware of everything scheduled to happen throughout the week.

Dr. Vinson got off his knees and sat down on the side of my bed so we could talk further about what the Warden intended to do now. I asked him how many other people were sick. He said that nearly 85 percent of the camp was sick, including some of his colleagues, but he, along with the Warden, some of the officers, and other staff members, was not affected by the food or water. He said the Warden suspected somebody had deliberately poisoned the food or the water so the project could be delayed or stopped altogether. Currently, his prime suspect was Mr. Townsend. The Warden couldn't prove he did it, but if he did do it, he had to have some help because there were too many refrigeration units for him to poison all the food by himself. It would be easier if he and his cohorts just poisoned the water because we only had four water storage units. Whatever the case was, the Warden intended to get down to the bottom of it because now the project had to be delayed until all the food and water was thoroughly checked. This culprit had the potential to put our work behind by nearly a week. If we didn't catch up, the Warden was going to be forced to tell the governor that something went wrong at the site, and he wanted to avoid as much as possible bringing the governor or the governor's spies in to snoop around.

Yawning, I asked Dr. Vinson if the medical staff had any vaccines or medication they were giving to any of the people who became sick. He said they tested hundreds of inmates who were sick, but all of their toxicology screens came back negative for toxins. The only thing they could infer was that we all had food poisoning. Dr. Vinson then asked me if I felt up to getting dressed and walking around to get some fresh air. After eating and taking in some fluids, I did begin to feel more energetic, so I told him I needed to shower first, but he could wait for me in my tent if he didn't have to do anything and we could stroll around when I came back. He said he would come back to get me in half an hour. He needed to check on something with the Warden first, but it wouldn't take long. I told Dr. Vinson I would be ready when he came back. I wanted to know what was going on, and I knew Dr. Vinson was going to get some information from the Warden that nobody else knew about yet. He was just that kind of guy.

Dr. Vinson came back as he promised and I was dressed and ready to go. I filled my knapsack with oranges and bottles of water that I brought from home so I could hydrate and energize myself while we were out. Other than the soup and soda, the last meal I remembered eating was the burger and fries Dr. Vinson had brought me Friday night. I needed to eat something, but I was skeptical about eating anything else because I didn't want to get any sicker than I had already been. I knew the oranges were safe because I didn't get them from the dining pavilion, so they were going to serve as lunch and dinner for today at least. Dr. Vinson and I took the scenic route to the main control unit, and the camp looked like a ghost town. There was no music, no leisure activities going on, no showers running, and there were no childish conversations to overhear between the inmates. Most of them were sick and in bed fighting to recover. Occasionally, an inmate or two would run out to the tree line to vomit or scurry along to the bathroom because they had diarrhea, but all else was quiet.

We entered the main control unit, and the Warden was sitting at the rectangular table sipping coffee, looking preoccupied and perplexed. When he saw me come in, he immediately stood up and asked me if I was all right while he offered to get me something to snack on or to drink. I told the Warden I was feeling a lot better, but I didn't remember much of anything that happened before today. Dr. Vinson pulled a chair out for me and we both sat down at the table with the Warden to listen to him. He said this unknown sickness started coming on sometime Sunday morning, or at least that's when the doctors' got their first case. The Warden said a contract worker on the western side of the camp began complaining about extreme stomach pain and nausea. The worker had a mild fever that seemed to gradually get worse as the doctor examined him. The doctor prescribed something to reduce the fever and eliminate the stomachaches and gave the worker some general-purpose advice on what to do over the next few days if his condition didn't improve. A few hours later, the worker came back with the same symptoms, but this time his fever was so high that they had to set him in a tub of ice.

Initially, the doctor thought maybe the worker was having an allergic reaction to something he didn't know he was allergic to, which could have been food, an insect bite, or some plants he had contact with out in the woods. The Warden said they waited until his fever went down before they took him out of the ice and placed him on his cot. They undressed the worker and checked his body for hives, welts, swelling and redness, and any other obvious signs of allergy or possible irritation. They didn't find a single thing, but the worker was too delirious to tell them what he had been doing before he felt sick. The doctor took some blood and urine samples from the worker, but all the tests came back negative. The only thing they knew was that they had an extremely sick worker who may or may not have been suffering from food poisoning. Since they didn't have the equipment to conduct more extensive tests, the Warden said he made a call to a personal friend in the nearby town who worked at the hospital. He and one of the doctors secretly took the worker to the hospital to have him examined. The test results were all the same; other than possible food poisoning, they couldn't find anything wrong with the man. The hospital staff released him and told the doctor and the Warden to just do what they had already been doing, and make sure the worker was rested because he was going to be weak from his fever. The Warden said he and the doctor left the hospital thinking it was going to be an isolated incident, but when they got back to the camp, they were hit with an epidemic.

I asked the Warden what his next move was, and he said he had already called in a team of inspectors to come and test the water first because that seemed like the most logical means of contamination. I asked him if he was going to have the food checked too, and he said he would consider it as a last resort only because it was nearly impossible for anybody to poison the food. He said there were only three people at the campsite who had keys or access to all the storage lockers: the chief of the contracted security team, Sergeant Thomas, who was currently suspended, and the Warden himself. The security officers had to lock and unlock the food storage units every day on every shift. When they locked the units up, their keys were put in a digital safe in the main control unit. The safe was set on a timer that allowed the security guards access only at the time designated for them to unlock the storage units for the next shift. Dr. Vinson told the Warden it was possible that whoever conspired to do this poisoned the food after it was already cooked. The Warden agreed and said it was possible but not likely. I asked him why it wasn't likely, and he said if the food was poisoned after it was cooked, then some, if not all of the cooks, should be sick because they usually taste the food as they cook it to add ingredients, but none of the cooks were sick. The food couldn't have been spoiled because it's kept frozen in the storage lockers until they decide to thaw it for the next day's meal.

We sat there silently for a little while, but deep down inside, we all wanted to talk about the clearing because it was becoming more obvious as each day passed that something sinister was looming in the atmosphere. We didn't want to empower the situation, but we didn't have a lot of answers to explain why all of these mysterious things began to happen, and it wasn't just the fact that they were mysterious. They were events that defied human logic. How can birds exposed to the same elements die only in a select area, and how is it possible for an entire camp to be poisoned by food except for the cooks who prepared the food? None of these things were rational, but trying to explain this to the governor or perhaps the general public would be a difficult task that we weren't ready to take on yet, so we continued playing the hand we were dealt.

Meanwhile, the inspectors showed up so they could start testing the water and the food. The leader of the team was a middle-aged man named Mr. Carter. The Warden received them into the main control unit and asked them to sit down so he could explain why he was having the water and food checked. Dr. Vinson and I stayed for the meeting and served hot coffee and store-bought cookies to our guest. The Warden introduced us as members of his consultative staff and told the inspectors we would accompany them to the storage lockers and the water containers for security purposes. The Warden didn't tell us before the inspectors arrived that he wanted me and Dr. Vinson to tag along with them, but he must have been reading our minds because we were planning on asking him if we could go with them anyway. We were just as eager to find out what was wrong with the water and the food as he was. Besides, there were so many food containers that it would take hours for them to inspect them all if the Warden didn't split them up in separate teams.

The Warden briefed the inspectors on why they were there and walked them next door to the lab with Dr. Vinson. They could change clothes and Dr. Vinson could show them what lab equipment we had in case they needed to run some tests. When they left the tent, the Warden used the combination to open the safe and retrieve the two other sets of storage unit keys for Dr. Vinson and me. The Warden told me again he was glad I was doing better and said for a moment, he thought he was going to have to call my father because my fever had gotten pretty high. I thought to myself that must have been why I didn't remember much about what happened over the weekend; I had probably lost consciousness.

The Warden said Dr. Vinson took a personal oath to check on me at least once every hour to gauge my progress. My fever had been quite high, and they were concerned that if it got any higher, I might convulse or have seizures. They used ice to bring my temperature down, but they didn't have to set me in a tub of it. The Warden even said that although he's not a religious man, he actually said a prayer on my behalf. I hugged the Warden and thanked him for ensuring my care and for praying for me. I told him he was like a big brother to me and that when this project business was over, we all had to go on vacation together. He burst out with laughter, saying he didn't need a vacation; he needed to retire.

Dr. Vinson came back with the inspection team all suited up and ready to go. The Warden told us to change the channel on our radios so the other officers or staff members wouldn't hear our communication. For the time being, he didn't want anybody else to know we had inspectors on the premises until we got the test results back. He told us to meet him back in the lab when we finished as well. If his team finished first, they would wait for us until we got there. Dr. Vinson and I agreed and took our team to inspect the units on the northern and eastern sides of the camp and the Warden's team inspected the western and southern sides of the camp.   Since most of the inmates and workers were sick and bedridden, there was little risk involved with being seen.

We started with the northern units first because they were further away from the lab. The inspectors climbed on top of the huge water container to remove the lid. One of the team members filled three small jars with water and then dropped different colored pills in each jar to see if the water would react to the pills. The other inspector stuck a chemical strip inside the water storage unit to test its acidity. He pulled that strip out and sealed it in a zip lock bag. He then stuck another strip in the water and waited for it to turn a certain color. He also stuck a rod as long as a yardstick into the container to test the water toward the bottom of the container as he had done the water on the top surface. When he finished, he pulled the rod out, and it too was sealed in an airproof bag. The two men climbed down and a third team member climbed up on top of the container and pulled out a bag with some big pills that resembled Alka-Seltzer drops. She dropped the pills in the water individually and in five-minute intervals. When the last pill was dropped, she climbed down and compared information with her other team members. We then went to the water storage container on the eastern side of the camp and they repeated the same steps. The entire process took a little over an hour and then we went back to the lab to meet up with the Warden.

The inspectors set their water samples aside long enough to remove their gloves and sit down at the table in the center of the room. One by one, each inspector presented us with their test results and explained what the colors on the chemical strip tests represented. They educated us on how water could be contaminated and what they were looking for specifically that would have indicated our water was polluted. When they all finished speaking, the verdict was rendered: our water wasn't contaminated. We were relieved and troubled all at the same time because now we had to check the food units. If the food wasn't contaminated, then the inspectors had the legal right to have our area quarantined for further testing to ensure this unknown sickness wasn't the result of a contagious, undiscovered biohazard.

As much as the Warden wanted the water to be the cause, he was crossing his fingers now hoping that it was the food. At least then we would have a legitimate reason for being behind that would shut Mr. Townsend up if the governor needed an explanation. More than that, we would have something scientific the inspectors could blame for the sickness. If the food was bad, the blame could be shifted to anybody from the pickers to the packers to the cooks, but the Warden didn't have to fear being personally blamed anymore, which made him feel a little better about the situation. The mere thought of having to tell anybody about the clearing was dreadful, so as long as these evil powers used something or did something that could be connected to something tangible, visible, or scientific, the Warden was in a better position.

We sat in the lab another twenty to thirty minutes, discussing the inspectors' results and trying to disguise our worry. They asked us how many days had passed since the sickness began attacking workers in our camp, and Dr. Vinson, always calm and poised, told them the first occurrences happened suddenly within the last twenty-four hours. He knew enough about the medical field not to say something that might cause the inspectors to believe there was possibly an airborne pathogen circulating in our camp. Since we were all contained miles away from other people, when the last person at our site got sick, no one else could be infected. The inspectors knew that and would probably indicate that in their final report, which meant that although most of the people in our camp were sick, we were essentially safe and there was no need to panic. That is what we wanted them to believe, but that is not how it really was. The Warden took a huge risk calling the inspectors out to the camp, but if he hadn't call them and the food or water really was contaminated, he could've been fined and fired. There was a fifty-fifty chance this situation could go in either direction. We just had to figure out which direction it would go in with the food now.

We left the lab with our teams, ready to inspect the food lockers. Dr. Vinson and I took our team back to the north location first as we had done the time before. We really didn't know what to expect but were hoping for something a little out of the ordinary. We opened all four of the refrigerated boxcars on the north side of the camp, and the inspectors walked inside with their biohazard suits, booties, and gloves. They had a box with thermometers and other gadgets they needed to use to test the food. When they finished inspecting the food inside the lockers, we closed and locked the doors, and they checked the hoses and gauges outside the lockers. They tested the reefer motors and even checked the fuel used to keep the motors running. When they finished their inspection, they jotted down some notes and we took them to the refrigerated boxcars on the eastern side of the camp to conduct the same tests. They didn't find anything wrong with the storage units on the northern and eastern sides of the camp. However, the Warden called us on the radio to meet him at the food lockers on the southern side of the camp — the side closest to the clearing.

When we met up with the Warden, his team of inspectors was checking the last food storage locker on the southern side. The lockers on the west side had all been cleared. When we got close enough to read the Warden's facial expression, he said that the inspectors had found the source of contamination and warned Dr. Vinson and me to stand back because there were live rodents in the locker. The inspectors from our team joined their colleagues in the locker while we stood outside about ten to fifteen feet away. The Warden told Dr. Vinson and me that somebody must have left the locker open because there were rats in that locker that had been eating and defecating and we could use our imaginations to fill in the rest. The inspectors didn't stay in the locker too long because the rats were running around trying to produce some body heat. The reefer was still pumping out a lot of cold air to keep the food frozen.

When the inspectors came out, they said with conviction they had no doubt now we were sick because we had probably come in contact with some bacteria from the rodents in that locker. There was no reason for them to search further, so they were going to write their final report for the Warden indicating that this storage locker had been accidentally left open, but all the other lockers were properly sealed and up to code. The Warden thanked them for coming out and offered to take them to dinner in town. They respectfully declined because they had another inspection to do this evening and had to drive three hours to get there. The inspectors wanted to hit the road as soon as possible so they could reach their destination before dark. We walked them back to the main control unit and waited for the report. We then walked them back to their van and waved as they drove off.

We were so relieved that was over, but we were curious to know how the rats got into the locker. It was always kept locked with limited access to the keys. Once the cooks took out the meat to be prepared for the next day's meal, the locker was shut and padlocked. Apparently we had some slackers working on the security team who left the lockers open and made all of us sick. The Warden despised shammers who didn't do their jobs. Now we were going to have to wait another three or four days for everybody to recover and that refrigerated boxcar had to be hauled out, rats and all. Another storage unit of food would have to be brought in to replace the contaminated one. He was glad there was a reasonable explanation for the sickness, but the Warden was furious the locker was left open because somebody could have died. He was not going to let the matter rest until he had a word with the chief security officer.

Once the inspectors were out of sight, the Warden stormed into the security tent, yelling for the chief. The chief came in quickly, but he, too, was sick and bent over. The Warden lit him up about leaving the storage locker open on the south end, but he swore he didn't do it. The Warden said some harsh but meaningless things to him and then left his tent. When the Warden came back outside, Dr. Vinson asked him if he believed the security chief had left the locker open. He said he knew the chief hadn't left it open, but he had already started yelling at him; he couldn't change directions midstream. I asked the Warden how he knew the chief was innocent, and he said the reefer was set at about thirty degrees. Even if the chief had left the locker open too long yesterday and then closed it later, the rats would still be frozen by now. Those rats weren't even shivering when the locker was opened for the inspectors. They looked like they had just come in. We didn't ask the Warden any more questions.

It was beginning to get dark now, so we headed back to the main control unit. The Warden needed to call the food packaging company to request another storage locker of food before they closed for the day. He also had to call a biohazard organization to have the rat-infested locker removed from the site. When he got off the phone, he said the biohazard group agreed to pick up the locker tonight and would be arriving in an hour. Dr. Vinson and I had to meet them on the main road and guide them through the camp to the lockers. All vehicles coming through the camp had to have ground guides regardless of what time they came or went.

About this time, Mr. Townsend awoke from his drug-induced coma and started walking around. He noticed the dining pavilions were all closed and no one else was walking around the camp. He came to the main control unit and started asking the Warden questions about why it was so quiet and why there was no food prepared at the dining pavilions. The Warden knew that no matter what he said, Mr. Townsend's paranoia was going to kick in and he was going to make a scene. He tried to give Mr. Townsend quick one-word responses without being obviously curt, but Mr. Townsend's incessant questions irked the Warden so much that he finally got up and punched Mr. Townsend in the mouth and walked out of the tent. Blood began to trickle down Mr. Townsend's shirt and one of his teeth fell out of his mouth. Dr. Vinson dipped his handkerchief in some water and offered it to Mr. Townsend, who was now cursing nonstop with a new lisp created by the missing tooth.

Mr. Townsend stormed out of the tent behind the Warden, all the while threatening to have the governor fire him. Dr. Vinson told Mr. Townsend this was not a good time to disturb the Warden and that he should go back to his tent and rest. Mr. Townsend refused to hear Dr. Vinson and continued pursuing the Warden. When they finally reached the edge of the camp where they could no longer be seen and could scarcely be heard, the Warden grabbed Mr. Townsend by his throat and told him in an even but low tone of voice that he was right about the clearing, but there was nothing that could be done about it. The Warden said all he wanted to do now was just finish the project as quickly as possible and leave; he didn't want any more outbursts from Mr. Townsend to disturb his peace. He asked Mr. Townsend if he understood what he was saying to him. The Warden was literally choking Mr. Townsend, so he couldn't breathe well enough to answer. The Warden told him to nod if he understood, so he started nodding while he tried to loosen the Warden's grip around his neck. The Warden wasn't going to kill him, but he wanted to get his point across rather emphatically. He kept choking Mr. Townsend until his face became flush and his struggle to breathe became less violent, then he let him go and left him coughing on the ground.

Dr. Vinson and I were waiting for the biohazard group to arrive. The Warden passed us on his way to his own tent. Dr. Vinson gave him a certain look, and the Warden said Mr. Townsend was still alive. Dr. Vinson smiled and we walked out to the edge of the camp to get Mr. Townsend. Dr. Vinson knelt down in front of him asked him if he was ready to go back to his tent now. Mr. Townsend nodded. We helped him up and brushed him off. He was still coughing and grabbing his neck where the Warden's hand had left a remarkable impression. Dr. Vinson told Mr. Townsend that no food had been cooked because nearly everybody in the camp was sick. One of the food lockers was left open and rodents got into it. We didn't know which one was bad until the Warden had them inspected today. Mr. Townsend was trying to talk but was still short of breath. Dr. Vinson told him not to worry because the locker was being picked up tonight. Mr. Townsend managed to eke out a few words between coughs, saying the locker was a small thing. We really needed to leave the area. Otherwise, something worse might happen.

Mr. Townsend was right. We did need to leave, but we couldn't. It was his fault. If he had listened to us before, maybe this could have been avoided, but we were knee deep in it now. Every day was going to present us with a new, unforeseen challenge we may or may not be able to deal with. These forces seemed to be getting angrier and more aggressive the longer we were out there. First, it was the birds, but it was relatively easy to get passed that because nobody got sick or died from them. But now, these spirits were doing things that had a direct physical effect on us. Any one of us could have died from the sickness or the rats. How would that be explained to the governor, our families, or the public? The only thing we could do now was just pray nobody got injured or killed while we were there because we couldn't defend ourselves against something we couldn't see.

CHAPTER TWELVE

Another week had passed, but we had fallen even further behind on our work because of the mysterious sickness that blindsided us all. The Warden had the food locker replaced, but he knew the angry spirits were behind it. The workers were finally recovering and the cooks were back on duty again. Everything seemed as if it was going back to normal, but we weren't counting our chickens before they hatched. The Warden told all the site supervisors to work at a swift but safe pace that was going to allow them to catch up gradually. We had a good three years to work on this project, so they didn't need to get in too big a hurry trying to finish. He also assured them they would still have all the time off that they were supposed to be allotted, so they didn't need to worry about being forced to work on their off days or on holidays. Last, he told them to do a visual inspection of their work areas and equipment. We were going to resume work tomorrow, and the Warden wanted to make sure all the equipment was topped off with fuel and in excellent working condition the way that it was when it was last used. The supervisors followed the Warden's orders and began checking their work areas and equipment and filled all the heavy equipment up to the brim with fuel so they would be ready for work first thing in the morning.

The Warden called a meeting for the committee members, which Mr. Townsend attended uninvited. The Warden wanted to let all the committee members know what had happened with the food and how the issue was resolved. He also told us the doctors would be distributing medical supplements for nausea and other food poisoning symptoms that could be taken on a voluntary basis by anyone who wanted them. The Warden told us about our anticipated work plan for the week and said he wanted us to meet again by this weekend to give all the committee members an opportunity to voice their opinions about our overall progress and make plans for our next work week.

Mr. Townsend couldn't wait for the Warden to finish before he blurted out what he wanted to say about the clearing, which created a lot of tension in the room. We all knew about the clearing, but only a few of the committee members consciously attributed the food poisoning issue to the clearing because the Warden found rats in the food locker. The Warden tried to talk over Mr. Townsend and continue on with what he wanted to say, but Mr. Townsend got even louder until passersby could hear what he said outside the tent. The Warden didn't want the inmates or contract workers to know what was going on, so he stopped speaking altogether so Mr. Townsend would bring his volume down.

However, the Warden did warn Mr. Townsend to be careful about what he said to the committee and anybody else at the campsite. He didn't want any vigilante groups to arise and attempt escape, but Mr. Townsend disagreed with the Warden and told him and us that the inmates and contract workers had a right to know that there were evil spirits within our camp. Agent Alvarez agreed with Mr. Townsend and said if the Warden and the committee members didn't tell everybody at the camp about the clearing soon then he and Mr. Townsend would. The two men walked out of the tent together, leaving the Warden and the other committee members in another compromising position.

Dr. Vinson asked the other FBI agents if they had known before now that Agent Alvarez was conspiring with Mr. Townsend. The other agents said they weren't aware Agent Alvarez and Mr. Townsend even knew each other. The Warden then asked them if they knew Agent Alvarez was related to Cobra, the leader of Los Serpientes. Agents Trevino and Ducati asked the Warden if he was sure Alvarez was related to or associated with Cobra. The Warden said he was sure, and Chaplain Beasley told the agents how we found out. Agent Trevino then said he had been trying to piece some things together since he and Ducati had been working undercover within Los Serpientes.

He kept trying to figure out how it was possible for the Snakes to always be one step ahead of the FBI with their movements. He said every time he phoned in a possible delivery of drugs or weapons, Los Serpientes would find out and change the location, sending the FBI on a wild goose chase. He said the only way they could've known was if someone on the inside was telling them, but for years the FBI couldn't figure out who it was because they limited access to the case against Los Serpientes to a few select agents who rarely had direct contact with the gang. Now it all made sense because Alvarez was one of few agents who worked undercover on the case. He was chosen because he spoke fluent Spanish and knew some of the informants who were either former members of the gang or worked with them in some capacity. The Warden made it official to the agents that Alvarez was the mole.

Agents Trevino and Ducati said we needed to lay a trap so we could catch Alvarez without him finding out that we knew about his relationship with Cobra. The Warden told the agents to leave that up to him. He said the quickest way to get people to talk in a prison was to spread a rumor. He said he would gladly lay the trap and would even bring Cobra in on it without letting him know he was being used. Chaplain Beasley interjected that all of that was well and good, but we still had to deal with the issues from the clearing. We couldn't deny all of these strange events were the results of us stirring up the dead. Dr. Vinson agreed and said we had to find a way to stop all of this. Agent Ducati asked the Warden if anybody had made contact with the Shaman yet. The Warden said he had planned on sending Dr. Vinson, and me but our trip had been delayed by the sickness. However, he was going to call the warden at that unit in Kansas to arrange a visit this week. The Warden then asked the committee members if we had anything further to suggest at the moment. We were all comfortable with the plans the Warden wanted to set in motion, so he concluded the meeting so we could get some rest and start fresh the next day.

At 4:30 the next morning, the Warden and several officers staged a surprised shakedown at the camp, and it was truly a surprise because the Warden didn't even tell the committee members he was going to do it. They bomb rushed the tents with bullhorns, flashlights, and canines. All the sleepy inmates and contract workers were dragged out of their tents in the early morning darkness before any of them had a chance to conceal anything or go to the bathroom. The Warden said he had reason to suspect somebody had contraband at his campsite, and when he found out who it was, they were going to be severely punished. He had the canines sniff everywhere while the officers turned everything upside down in tent city until they found the lone marijuana cigarette he had planted in Cobra's duffle bag.

Cobra started cursing and denying the joint was his. He pleaded with the Warden, saying somebody was setting him up. Of course, the Warden knew that because he was the one who had the joint planted in Cobra's bag to begin with. It was all part of the Warden's plan. Needless to say, the Warden had Cobra shackled and hauled into the main control unit so he could isolate him long enough to talk to him. It was the only way he could keep his conversation with Cobra a complete secret. In the meantime, everybody else had to stand outside their tents and wait for the officers to finish the shakedown before they could go anywhere, including Mr. Townsend and the undercover agents.

The Warden had a couple of officers posted outside the main control unit while he spoke privately to Cobra in the tent. He asked Cobra if he felt he could trust anybody at the prison.

Cobra told the Warden he learned as a young boy that you could only trust people as far as you can see them. The Warden asked Cobra if he trusted him. Confused, Cobra hesitantly stated he didn't understand. The Warden said he was aware of that, but he was going to explain some things to him that would add clarity to the situation. When he finished explaining then they would both have a clear understanding of each other. Cobra told the Warden he was all ears. Smiling, the Warden admitted he had the joint planted in his bag because he needed to talk to him alone without drawing any unnecessary attention to them. Cobra probed the Warden to find out what was so important he had to plant drugs on him just to talk to him alone. The Warden responded that he knew Agent Alvarez was a dirty agent who was working with Los

Serpientes and that was how they managed to avoid being caught. Agent Alvarez was telling Los Serpientes everything the FBI was doing. Cobra didn't say anything. The Warden proceeded to tell Cobra further that he also knew Cobra and Alvarez were related through marriage. They personally knew each other so when they saw each other back at the compound, Cobra knew right away that he was being watched closely.

Cobra snapped it wasn't his fault if Alvarez was willing to risk his job. The Warden retorted that Cobra was right — it wasn't his fault. However, Alvarez wasn't going to risk his job anymore. The Warden made it seem as if Alvarez was about to set Cobra up for a big fall. Since he was already locked up, they were going to add so much more time to his sentence that he would never see daylight as a free man. Angry now, Cobra responded it wasn't right because he wasn't the one calling the shots anymore. Alvarez called all the shots because he used all of Los Serpientes' street contacts and he had the FBI on his side. Cobra said he wasn't voluntarily working with Alvarez. Alvarez threatened to expose everybody he knew from politicians to cartel members to dirty cops. He had them all where he wanted them. The Warden made it plain to Cobra that he had to tell him everything if he wanted some help getting out of this mess. Cobra told the Warden that Alvarez would have him killed if he talked. The Warden stated he might have him killed too if he didn't talk, so it was his decision about who he was going to trust. He had twenty-four hours to decide what he wanted to do. Otherwise, he was going to find himself in a worse situation.

The Warden waited until after the shakedown was over to release Cobra back into the general population. The shakedown lasted about three hours. Everybody at the camp was abruptly awakened by the sound of barking dogs and officers on the bullhorns. Afterward, we all got dressed and filed into the dining facilities so we could start going our separate ways when breakfast was over. The Warden called the committee members on the radio for an unscheduled meeting at 9:00 AM. By that time, all the workers would be in their areas working and we could have some privacy. Dr. Vinson and his colleagues met up with me at the dining pavilion on the north side of the camp for breakfast. Naturally, we planned to discuss the surprise shakedown. It was a brilliant tactic, and we had a feeling we were going to find out at this morning's meeting just how effective it was.

We sat down at a table in the back as we normally did, enjoying our breakfast and passing the time with stimulating conversation. For the first time in several days, we felt we could breathe easy. Nothing was exactly normal, but it was closer to being normal today than it had been in nearly a week. The sickness was gone, the rat-infested food trailer had been taken away, and the sound of heavy equipment began filling the air today as it had a couple of weeks ago. We thought maybe the gods were going to have a little mercy on us for at least a day because everything started off right today. On the previous occasions, when these angry spirits did something, it was usually already done by the time we got up in the morning. But this morning was different. The only things stirring before the day began this time was the Warden and the canines. We all had to admit it felt good to walk outside the tents this morning and see nothing but dirt on the ground, and nobody was sick either. But just when we thought things could get no worse, one of the officers called out on the radio. There was an emergency on the south side of the camp.

Dr. Vinson, his colleagues, and I ran from the northern dining pavilion through the center of the camp to the project site on the south side. The Warden, Mr. Townsend, and the other committee members were already there when we arrived. Some of the inmates had to be taken away from the site because they were vomiting and some of them had even fainted. We made our way to the front of the crowd that had gathered and formed a horseshoe around the area. I went and stood by the Warden to show some solidarity. The Warden had the site supervisors split their workers up in three equal groups so they could continue working on the project in the other three corners of the campsite. After all the workers were marched away, nobody was left standing except the committee members, Mr. Townsend, the FBI agents, the scientists, and the Warden.

The workers and heavy equipment operators on the south side had finally reached the clearing, the place where all the mysterious occurrences originated. None of the workers or inmates knew anything about it, and we thought it best not to tell them. But our secret place was no longer a secret, and even though the workers didn't know anything about what had happened there centuries ago, they knew this mystical area was dangerous because they too saw some new dead bodies with the missing torsos. They didn't the see the bodies we saw several months ago when the pictures of the politicians were disseminated throughout prisons in the nation. They didn't see the dead bodies Dr. Vinson had warned us about in his presentation. They didn't see the dead bodies on the streets during the riots, but they had seen the dead bodies at the clearing today because they were scattered all over the entire area.

Mr. Townsend started shouting and making a commotion about the dead bodies we were gazing at on the ground. He ran up to the Warden and yelled repeatedly that he needed to stop this project because there were demons in the woods that were going to kill us. The Warden had to call some officers in to drag Mr. Townsend away from the clearing because he was going into hysterics. The rest of us stood there, forcing ourselves to not make comments about what we were seeing. The

Warden finally succumbed to what seemed to be the inevitable and said it was time to call the governor. Dr. Vinson and the other scientists agreed but told us to not touch anything this time. They also suggested there had to be a portal nearby, and it was crucial that we found it. That was the only way these bodies could've been dismembered without any blood being on the ground; they had to be thrown through the portal.

They told us to pick up some small rocks and form a horizontal line with the starting point beginning on the left side of the Warden. We all filled both of our hands and all of our pockets with as many small rocks as we could find. We formed a line standing shoulder to shoulder starting at the Warden's left shoulder. Dr. Vinson told each of us to throw one rock a few feet in front of us starting with the Warden and ending with the last person standing in line. If the rock hit the ground, we were to repeat the same process after taking two steps forward. After we found our places in the line, we all threw a rock the first time, but nothing happened. We were surprised but not overwhelmed because we figured it was possible we were throwing rocks in the wrong direction or maybe we just didn't throw them far enough, so we all threw a second rock.

After this round of rock throwing, we were beginning to wonder if maybe the scientists were wrong because nothing happened again, but it did seem logical that the bodies were thrown from a portal somewhere close by because there was no blood on the ground, and there were no skid marks or other signs that they were drug into that location from some other place. The Warden was just about ready to give up and told all of us if nothing happened after this next round, we would just call it a day and go back to the main control unit to wait for orders from the governor. We mutually agreed this would be our last round, so one by one we all started throwing our rocks. Eighteen people were standing in line, with the addition of the scientists and the Warden. The Warden threw his rock and got no response. I threw mine next and got no response and so on, and so on, and so on until the ninth person threw the rock.

Chaplain Beasley happened to be the ninth person standing in the line. When he threw his rock, it disappeared. Suddenly, we were all filled with wonder and horror by the fact that we had found an opening to another dimension. Dr. Vinson told him to throw another rock, and the second one disappeared also. Dr. Vinson told him to throw a third rock but at a shorter distance than he had thrown the previous one. We had found the portal, but Dr. Vinson said we needed to leave some kind of mark on the ground so we would know where it was. Chaplain Beasley threw a third rock just shy of the portal, and Dr. Vinson drew a line and placed some sticks on the ground forming an arrow so we could get to the portal because now that we knew where it was, we had to find a way to destroy it.

Agent Alvarez told the Warden he was insane if he remotely considered going inside that portal at all, but the Warden said it might be our only hope. Even if we left the campsite, the portal would remain open and all hell would break loose. If there was a way to close the portal, we had to find it. Alvarez argued we would be committing suicide if we went inside that portal. We didn't know what we were up against. We didn't know how many gods or spirits or people were in that dimension. We didn't know anything. The Warden told Alvarez he didn't need to be concerned about the portal because he wasn't traveling inside of it anyway; he needed to focus his attention on finding a good lawyer who could put up a strong argument at the sentencing phase of his trial. Alvarez was stunned and so were we. The Warden told Alvarez in front of all of us that he knew Alvarez was the mole in the FBI and he was the one calling the shots on the streets. Alvarez was using Cobra and setting him up to be the fall guy the entire time. The other agents told Alvarez that when the governor came, they were going to have him taken into custody and locked up. Alvarez took off running, but the Warden told the others not to chase him because we were in an isolated area. There was nowhere he could go. Besides, the security detail would catch him if he tried to leave the camp.

The Warden told the officers who were committee members to have the area completely secured. No one was to go to the clearing for any reason. The officers radioed for help to get the heavy equipment moved back to the staging area. Once the equipment was moved, they wrapped the trees with tape so everyone would know that area was off limits. The Warden called all of his officers on the radio and had them march the inmates who lived on the south side back to the area so they pack and relocate until we left the campsite for good. While they were packing and moving, the Warden told Dr. Vinson and me to pack a bag because we were catching the next flight to Kansas to see the Shaman. Ducati insisted the Warden allow him to accompany us because he had dealt with the Shaman before and knew his tricks. Chaplain Beasley also urged the Warden to let Ducati go because he said the Shaman did have some special powers he used against people if he sensed fear in them or if he thought he was being taken advantage of. The Warden acquiesced but told Agent Ducati to make sure he called his superiors to let them know what was happening before he went to Kansas. He could get clearance for Dr. Vinson and me, but he didn't have the authority to clear a federal agent.

The Warden called the unit in Kansas and briefed the officers on why he was sending two people from his Special Crimes Committee to see the Shaman. The officers told the Warden they would make sure we had everything we needed when we arrived, but they also told the

Warden to make sure he told us not to touch the Shaman when we saw him because he possessed some dark powers that made people sick after they touched him. When the Warden hung up the phone, he called Agent Ducati to the main control unit to ask him about these powers the Shaman had that made people sick. Chaplain Beasley chimed in, reiterating what was said on the phone. Agent Ducati also affirmed what the Kansas officers said. He told the Warden that the Shaman had practiced witchcraft for a very long time and did possess certain powers, but it was mostly superstition. He was a master at taking advantage of what people feared. The Warden told us to take every precaution necessary and to follow whatever directives our Kansas friends gave us. He was counting on us to bring back help.

We were catching the early bird flight at 6:00 AM. The Warden thought it best to have us stay the night at a hotel in town next to the airport, since the closest city with an airport was two hours away. The Warden told us he had already made the security chief aware of what was happening, so they had a van already warmed up and waiting to take Dr. Vinson, Agent Ducati, and me to the airport. The Warden called the governor's office before we left. The governor and his council members were expected to arrive in a week. He was currently out of town on business. Now that Agent Alvarez knew we were on to him, there was only one thing left for him to do. He had to kill Cobra because he was the only person who could testify against him in court. Nobody else would testify against him because they stood to lose too much. On the other hand, Cobra had nothing to lose and everything to gain. If he gave the feds enough information, they might even let him out of prison, but Alvarez would be locked up for life. He couldn't let that happen. All of the other agents knew he was dirty, and no one would side up with him. The only person left for him to collude with was Mr. Townsend.

Agent Alvarez told Mr. Townsend bits and pieces of the ordeal between him and Cobra, but he also offered to give him a share of the profits he had been making on the streets if Mr. Townsend agreed to help him get rid of Cobra. The offer was tempting, but Mr. Townsend was a control freak and a scoundrel who didn't like to be part of a group unless he was leading it. He told Agent Alvarez that whatever they conspired to do had to be done his way; otherwise, Alvarez could find somebody else to do his dirty work for him. Alvarez didn't have a lot of time, and although he was calling the shots on the streets, his word meant nothing behind bars. If the members of Los Serpientes found out he was trying to kill Cobra, Alvarez would be tortured and killed himself. Cobra may have been Alvarez's puppet due to circumstances beyond his control, but Cobra was still a ruthless killer who made an example of people who betrayed him.

Alvarez agreed to go along with Mr. Townsend's plan as long as he didn't have to go court, lose his job, or serve any time. Mr. Townsend told Alvarez he would never have to worry about Cobra again because he was going to be executed or die on death row. He said that instead of taking a crazy risk like trying to kill Cobra, all they needed to do was blame him and his gang members for the murders to the governor. The governor already hated the fact that his state was housing the man and his gang. All he needed was a reason to execute them and it would be done. Alvarez asked Mr. Townsend if he was sure that his plan would work. Mr. Townsend told him not worry because he was the governor's right-hand man. The governor trusted him. He was going to tell the governor himself that the Warden was covering up for Cobra and his gang. They killed those politicians several months ago, and the proof was at the clearing. Mr. Townsend said he was going to show the governor the dead bodies with the missing torsos and that would convince him that Los Serpientes did it.

What Mr. Townsend didn't know was the Warden had already called the governor and told him the area was haunted just as the scientists said it was when they first discovered the clearing. There were unidentified dead bodies all over the place, and they were mutilated just like the politicians. The Warden had even told the governor that he tried to get Mr. Townsend to delay the project a little longer until they had more conclusive information about the former inhabitants of that region. He said if Mr. Townsend had listened to him, all the bad things that had happened could have been avoided. However, there was a way it could be stopped now. The governor agreed to hear the Warden out when he came to the campsite with his council members to determine what they needed to do for damage control, but he was also enraged when he found out what all Mr. Townsend had been doing. He told the Warden not to worry because he would take care of everything when he arrived. All that the Warden had to do was maintain control until then.

CHAPTER THIRTEEN

I should have been sleepy when we arrived at the Supermax in Kansas because I only slept about four hours. I kept thinking about what Chaplain Beasley and Agent Ducati said about the Shaman, so I had a lot of nervous energy. I had seen bizarre people behind bars before — Cobra was one of them — but I had never met anyone who supposedly possessed supernatural powers. If I had, I wasn't aware of it. We pulled up at the main gate, and the place looked like something from a movie. I had worked at a prison for over ten years, but I had never seen anything like this. There was so much barbed wire on top of barbed wire with wrought iron and cement bricks, and there was nothing but wide-open space around the whole place. They didn't even have trees growing on the yard or outside of the yard. It was just wide-open space with very little grass, and there were rows of something that the inmates had plowed in a nearby area separated by more barbed wire. There were no windows on the front of the building so none of the inmates could see who was coming in or who was going out. From a distance, it looked as if part of the prison was underground. As we got closer to the main building, I found out it was.

When we arrived, there were several stages of security we had to pass through. The first stage was outside of the building about fifty yards from the front door. We couldn't take our cell phones or keys and we couldn't take money in with us; that was standard procedure for a prison. However, the second phase of security was a lot more intense. We had to change shoes if we had worn shoes with laces. We could not wear a belt, and if we wearing hoodies, we had to take the drawstring out of the hood. I had to take my earrings out, and none of us could wear watches or jewelry of any kind. The last phase of security was more like a mini hygiene stop. We had to put on white jumpsuits, hairnets, safety glasses, and gloves. I asked the officers escorting us why we needed all of this, and they said the inmates on the wing where we were going had a tendency to throw their feces at people. They said the wing where the Shaman was located primarily housed criminals with psychiatric problems, so everybody had to wear safety gear to walk through that area.

We walked down a long corridor with white-washed brick walls, a stone gray cement floor, and huge flood lights fastened to the ceiling every so many feet. The place smelled like an old closet. It was dank and practically airtight since there were no windows on that level. None of the doors had knobs. You had to stick a key in the hole and then push the door open or shut. There were cameras everywhere and there were burglar bars and wires around the plumbing pipes and ventilations ducts in each room on that floor. We took the elevator down at least two stories to get to the block where the Shaman was located. One of the guards kept us in a holding room to give us specific instructions about how we were supposed to conduct ourselves with this inmate.

The officer told us not to answer any questions that weren't related to our case. He said that although the Shaman practiced "the craft," he was a very intelligent individual who worked as a psychiatrist before he was incarcerated. He knew how to look into the souls of people with his words. If you let him get inside of your mind, he could talk you into a trance and you would leave here with some evil seeds that he subliminally planted. The officer warned us about getting too comfortable with the Shaman. He claimed the Shaman had a way of making people feel welcomed when they came to see him. His congenial disposition made him easy to like, but he was just as cruel as he was hospitable and his cordiality was all part of a psychological game he played. Finally, he told us that no matter what the Shaman did or said, we could not have physical contact with him.

I asked the officer to elaborate on these powers the Shaman supposedly possessed because I wanted to know more about the inmate we were going to see. The officer asked me if I was sure I wanted to know, and Dr. Vinson and I looked at each and back at the officer. Dr. Vinson asked the officer if he had first-hand knowledge of these powers. The officer responded he had never seen anyone touch the Shaman before. However, he had seen several people, including news reporters, come in to interview him. Whenever they left, they all looked like they were older than they were when they arrived. Their skin was wrinkled, and some of them became feeble and had to be carried out. Agent Ducati told the officer he had worked on a case that involved the Shaman, and it was rumored he would take years of a person's life from them in exchange for information. The officer stated there was a strong possibility the rumor was true, which is why the Shaman lived on a cellblock in total isolation appropriately labeled "The Auction Block."

According to the officer, the Shaman's cellblock was given this name because visitors had to barter their time if they wanted information from him. The amount of time they gave him was determined by the amount of information they wanted. He didn't want money or material things. He was serving a multiple life sentence and knew he would never be physically free to enjoy those things. What he wanted was power, and as long as he continued living, he would remain powerful even in captivity. He was like a demigod. People consistently traveled thousands of miles just to interview this man, but he knew that one day, all of this would come to end because he had to die as all humans do. Until then, he continued exchanging information for time and his dark powers remained strong.

Naturally, when people come to see him, it is expected that they are prepared to sell him years from their lives for his information. If they are not willing to bargain, then he will shut down and force a standoff, especially if he knows the information is critical. They usually end up coming back, and the Shaman gets inside of their minds and eventually gains the time he wanted after all. The officer told us our best bet was to try to persuade him to think that although his help was being solicited, we had other options that might work if he refused to give his help. Agent Ducati said it might be worth the risk because we really needed to get some answers, and the Shaman was the most likely person who could give them to us. The officer recapped all the safety rules to us once more and finally turned the key and pushed the door open to the Auction Block.

We walked down a long, mildewed-smelling hallway with more cages and very little light, and it reminded me all over again of why I hated going to visit inmates in solitary confinement. There was a cell lit up at the end of the hallway, and you could hear music playing in the cell. The closer we got to the cell, the faint smell of flowers and food became stronger. All three of us carried our own chairs and the notepads and pens the officer had given us before he opened the door to this cellblock. Before we actually reached the cell, we heard what sounded like an argument between at least two people, but it was our assumption that the Shaman was alone. We stopped in the hallway and waited a few minutes. The Shaman already knew we were there and told us to come closer to his cell because everything was all right.

The voice we heard didn't sound like a voice belonging to a man that practiced witchcraft. It was calm and somewhat melodic. Listening to him was like listening to a father who had taken his seven-year-old son outside to teach him how to play football. It was like listening to a Sunday school teacher talking about Moses and Jesus. There was something honest about his voice, which it made difficult for me to imagine he was as evil as people said he was. I supposed that was another reason why he had to be kept in complete isolation. It was just like the officer said: if you listened to him long enough, he could persuade you to do something for him. It was a good tactic to gain people's trust. I could understand better now how a person might accede to his sophistication.

We sat our chairs down in front of the cell, but we couldn't see the Shaman. He had layers of fabric layered like curtain panels covering the door of his cell. Since he lived on that block alone, his cell didn't have a solid door that concealed everything. It was a regular cell with bars on the front. We imagined he was cooking or had cooked something because the cell and the hallway smelled like food. We also saw the potpourri boiler, which explained the smell of fresh flowers. We sat there and waited for the mystery man to appear, but he didn't come out right away. Agent Ducati got a little anxious and hollered for the Shaman to come out because we needed to talk to him about something important. The Shaman yelled back that he was almost done and would be with us in a few minutes.

When he pulled the string that drew his curtains back, he was sitting Indian-style on top of a weird looking rug that covered his cell floor. There was incense burning and something boiling on the electric burner he had on the floor on the opposite side of his cell. He was wearing solid colored pajamas or some kind of leisure outfit for men with a matching top and bottom. He was sitting down on the floor like he was meditating, but I couldn't tell if we were looking at his face or at the back of his head because he was clean shaven and had tattoos of eyes all over his head. He rose from the floor, and we could see then that he had tattoos of eyes everywhere, not just on his head. I thought Cobra looked freakish when I first saw him face to face, but he couldn't hold a candle to the Shaman.

The man finally stopped meditating, or whatever he was doing, and greeted us warmly. He cordially offered us something to drink, but we all politely refused. It was hard for me to focus on his conversation because he had so many tattoos of eyes all over him. I felt we were being watched by invisible beings and that made me uncomfortable. Those eyes made him look dirty and perverse, but outside of his witchcraft, he may have actually been a decent person. I know I shouldn't have been thinking about it at that moment, but I couldn't imagine a woman going to bed with this man with all those eyes tattooed everywhere. They were really getting under my skin, and I supposed Dr. Vinson could sense my irritation because he placed his right hand on top of my left hand and smiled. It helped me to calm down a little, but those eyes were extremely annoying, and in the back of my mind, I began to wonder if some of the spirits he worshipped were going to start touching me.

Apparently, Ducati and Dr. Vinson had already introduced themselves and told him who I was because he called me by my first name. I was so distracted by those eyes, and it seemed each eye had its own personality or its own voice that was whispering about us as we sat there. It was as if we were alien organisms being examined under a microscope. I felt as if this man was visually undressing me. I wanted to leave right then. I didn't care if we got information about the portal or not. Dr. Vinson asked me if I was okay. I said I was fine, but it was really stuffy in the hallway, and my allergies were acting up. The Shaman offered me some tissue just in case I started sneezing. I remembered what the officer said about touching him, so I declined the tissue but thanked him for his offer.

We finally got down to business and told the Shaman explicitly why we there. Dr. Vinson was not particularly impressed by the man but was willing to entertain him so we could get what we came for. Dr. Vinson told the Shaman we had opened a portal to another dimension — a dimension of Los Antiguos. He told him about the dead bodies with the missing torsos and all the other things that had befallen us. The Shaman stood up, placing his hands behind his back, and said he was possessed by a spirit that had come from that world, and he was not going to help us close the portal unless we brought him back with us so he could he rejoin his people in that dimension. Agent Ducati pressed the Shaman for help but also told him we weren't in a position to negotiate his release. The governor of Kansas had to arrange his transfer to our state. The Shaman reminded us he was serving a multiple life sentence. His point was that it would be cost-effective for them to just let him go instead wasting the taxpayers' money keeping him locked up until he ran out of time. The portal would be closed forever, and they would never see him again.

Dr. Vinson didn't like the fact the Shaman was taking advantage of us, but we didn't have a lot of options. We left the Supermax and went back to our hotel rooms. Dr. Vinson called the Warden and told him what happened. The Warden was flabbergasted but willing to try anything at this point because the spirits from the portal had brought hundreds of poisonous snakes into the camp since we had been gone and several people had been bitten. The Warden was tired and at his wits' end. He had done all he could do to keep that campsite secure, but he was facing something now that his military experience could not overcome. He assured us he would have an answer from the governor tonight and this would be resolved, so we sat tight and waited for the Warden's call.

The Warden called Dr. Vinson back about four o'clock in the morning. He made a conference call to our governor and the governor of Kansas. They reached an agreement to have the Shaman brought back with us so we could end this nightmare. The Warden explained the issue to the governor of Kansas, who was all too glad to unload the Shaman on us. The only thing they were working on now was finalizing the details of how we were going to transport him. The Shaman was too dangerous to be flown back on a commercial plane, and the drive back was too long for us to be alone with the man. No matter what idea they came up with, the Warden guaranteed that one way or the other, we would be on our way home today so we could check out of our hotel later that morning. Dr. Vinson gave Ducati and me the news. We packed up our things and rested until daylight.

Agent Jones from the U.S. Marshals' office knocked on my hotel door around 8:30 that morning. He showed me his badge and asked if I had some bags he could help me carry downstairs. We were being flown back by helicopter by the U.S. Marshals. It was the safest and most convenient means of travel we had available given the situation. When I got outside, there were two helicopters waiting. The helicopter carrying the Shaman was hovering above us a few feet in the air. The other was on the ground waiting for us to board so we could leave. Dr. Vinson had saved me a seat next to him on the eleven-seat helicopter. I got in, fastened my seat belt, and we took off.

We arrived at a helipad about two hours later. From there, we had another thirty-minute drive to the campsite, where the Warden and the governor were waiting for us. The Warden had already locked the camp down because of the snakes, so nobody was outside when we pulled up. The U.S. Marshals unloaded the Shaman, who was wrapped with chains from head to toe on something resembling a standing gurney with wheels. They introduced themselves to the governor and the Warden and asked where they needed to wheel the inmate. The Warden called some of the officers on the radio and told them to stand guard by the tape on the trees at the south side of the camp. He didn't tell them what we were doing. He simply said we would be back.

The governor introduced himself to the Shaman as the person responsible for his transfer. He asked him if he needed anything before we got started. The Shaman sincerely thanked the governor for being merciful. He was glad to finally be rejoining his people. He exclaimed it was a dream he never imagined would come true, but now that it was here, he was glad to go back to where he belonged and was willing help us close the portal permanently so no one could ever pass through again. His plan was to lead us inside the portal so we could destroy the killing ground. We had to burn it with fire, and the portal would be closed forever, as long as nobody picked up anything from that dimension and brought it back. The task sounded simple enough, but we wouldn't know how difficult it really was until we crossed over on the other side.

Dr. Vinson and I agreed to go with the Shaman, along with the scientists and some of the officers who were committee members. The Warden and the governor decided to wait back at the camp for us in case we needed backup. We set a time limit, which gave us an hour to get in and get out. The Shaman instructed all of us on what we might see when we crossed over, including his own personal transformation. Our mission was to encompass the clearing with a gasoline trail and set it on fire. Once the fire was lit, we would have a small window of time to come back through the portal. Dr. Vinson suggested we do the rock test again after we came out, and then we would know for sure that the portal was closed.

We all filled up a gas can and took matches and flares to start the fire. The U. S. Marshals took the chains off the Shaman, and he started transforming into a more primitive-looking being before our very eyes.

He indeed belonged to the world of Los Antiguos, a world we were too modernized to understand. It was a world that was called uncivilized because we didn't know anything about how they defined civilization. After working in the prison all these years, that world didn't seem so far apart anymore. Locking people up for decades at a time was just as much a form of human sacrifice as murder. We just didn't see it that way.

The Shaman entered the portal first and we followed closely behind him. When we got on the other side, the clearing looked nearly the same, except the trees and shrubs were completely overgrown because the crash course with Europeans and technology hadn't occurred yet. We began pouring gasoline around the portal so we could burn the area as instructed. The Shaman told us to hurry because he was changing rapidly and wasn't sure he could hold his original form back much longer. We had made it halfway around the portal when Mr. Townsend jumped through and fell on the ground in front of us. The officers drew their weapons and told him not to move, but Dr. Vinson suggested they let him go because he would never survive in this world. The officers laughed but managed to resist the temptation and held him at gunpoint until we were done. We lit the matches and set off the flares. The entire area went up in flames.

The scientists went back through the portal first. The officers followed them, throwing Mr. Townsend through the portal with them. Dr. Vinson and I were the last to go through, but before we went, we said our last good-byes to the Shaman. We extended our hands to him, but he initially refused to touch us. Dr. Vinson asked him what was wrong. The Shaman looked puzzled because we should've been afraid he would take some time from our lives if we touched him, but we were not. Dr. Vinson grabbed the Shaman's hand and shook it anyway and so did I. The Shaman said he never wanted to take time away from anybody else's life. He just wanted to live long enough to get his own life back. We understood and respected what he said because he didn't do anything different from any other inmate. They were all on an auction block, bartering time, talent, and resources for survival. That was just how prison life was, so we waved for the last time and jumped through the portal.

Everybody who had gone through the portal formed a straight-line, standing shoulder to shoulder as we had done before for the rock test. Each of us took turns throwing a rock to see if it would hit the ground; all the rocks hit the ground on the first try. We took two steps forward and threw another rock. They all hit the ground on the second attempt. We took two steps forward again and threw a third rock. When the last person's rock hit the ground on the third attempt, we all started celebrating right there in woods. We didn't know who killed those politicians, but at least we didn't have to worry about anything else coming from the portal. One of the officers called the Warden on the radio and told him that we made it. We were on way back to the main control unit.

By the time we got back, the U.S. Marshals had already cuffed Alvarez and shoved him in the back seat of their car. They were transporting him as a favor to the FBI since they were already at the camp. The governor told Mr. Townsend he was under arrest for being in cahoots with Alvarez to frame Cobra and Los Serpientes for the murders of the unidentified bodies found at the clearing. Therefore, Mr. Townsend was also handcuffed, but the Marshals only had one car and didn't want the men riding together, giving them an opportunity to change their stories, so the Warden agreed to keep Mr. Townsend locked up at the camp until the governor sent another unit to pick him up.

The governor's council members sat down with everybody involved with the clearing and told us what to say to the press if asked. Damage control was a big issue, especially since it was an election year. The governor told us we could have the rest of the week off, but work would resume next Monday. He thanked us for our hard work and diligence and then left with his council members. Exhausted but grateful this was finally over, Dr. Vinson, his colleagues, the Warden, and I decided to go eat as much as we could at the dining pavilion. We had been sitting on pins and needles ever since we discovered that clearing and none of us really had a healthy appetite, but we planned to make up for it tonight.

We all decided to go eat on the western side of the camp so we could stay out of the way. All the inmates who used to live on the south side of the camp had to move back, so some of them starting moving back after the governor left. They wanted to make the most of their time off. Tonight, the cooks were serving meatloaf, mashed potatoes with gravy, corn on the cob, and sweet peas. We were all excited about dinner and ready to eat. We moved through the line pretty quickly and found a table in the back where we would normally sit, enjoying our food and engaging in stimulating conversation. We were all in high spirits now and were making plans for long vacations when this was over.

One of the officers who had gone in the portal with us came over to talk and joke with us. We were getting a little rowdy and he could hear us in the back of the dining pavilion. He was telling us what Mr. Townsend was doing when he and another officer cuffed him to a streetlamp next to the security tent by the main road. The security detail didn't want him snooping around inside their tents no more than we wanted him around us, but they needed to bind him in a safe place. We all could picture Mr. Townsend trying to squirm out of the cuffs so we laughed at the thought of it. The officer continued on telling us he had to get one of the doctors to give Mr. Townsend a medical cocktail for him to calm down so they could search him. The officer was overcome with laughter when he pulled a small figure made of sticks and rags out of a bag he was carrying and set in on the table. He kept laughing but finally managed to say he got this doll out of Mr. Townsend's pocket.

Nobody was smiling anymore, and the only person laughing was the officer. Dr. Vinson asked the officer if Mr. Townsend told either of them where he got the doll. The officer was still laughing, asking us what kind of man carries a doll around in his pocket. The Warden pounded his fist on the table to get the officer's attention. He finally stopped laughing and started looking around at our faces that were showing signs of worry and panic all over again. The Warden asked him again if Mr. Townsend told him where he got the doll. Smiling, the officer said Mr. Townsend claimed he picked up the doll in the portal.